7/16

CONFUSION IS NOTHING NEW

PAUL ACAMPORA

CONFUSION IS NOTHING NEW

Scholastic Press / New York

For Debbie, Nicholas,
& Gabrielle

CHAPTER 1: GLOCKENSPIELS AND HAND GRENADES

It's Friday night football, late in the fourth quarter, and St. Francis of Assisi's Howling Wolves are on the verge of a perfect season. By perfect, I mean that our team has not won a single game. There's no way we're going to win this one either.

"Let's go, Wolf Pack!" hollers my best friend, Daniel Field.

"You might not have noticed," I say, "but we're down by forty with less than five minutes to go."

"Ellie," says Daniel, "they may be losers, but they're our losers."

Daniel stands in the Howling Wolf flute section on a metal bleacher behind me. We both play in the St. Francis Marching Band. Daniel's got a piccolo. I bang on a glockenspiel. Daniel would rather be the Howling Wolf mascot, but he's too short for the costume. I honestly don't know what I'd rather be doing right now because just before the game, my father informed me that my mother is dead.

"She can't be dead," I said when Dad shared the news.

My father stood near our kitchen sink, preparing ingredients for pumpkin soup. He barely looked up from his work. "Your mother doesn't need permission to be dead, Ellie."

"But I never even met her."

Dad slid a pile of potato peels onto an old copy of the *Rockhill Free Press* that would end up in his compost pile later. "Her loss. Not yours."

Wilma "Korky" Korkenderfer—aka my mom—left Dad and me just a few months after I was born and never came back again. That was fourteen years ago. Dad never forgave her. I never really missed her. That's probably because I never really knew her. Still, it's not like the woman who gave me life, big feet, and frizzy hair didn't exist. In my mind, she was something between a pope and a platypus. Definitely real but not something I expected to see in the yard any time soon. Still, meeting my mom in person was definitely on my list of things to do. At least one day.

"You don't think this is a big deal?" I asked my father.

Dad cut stalks off a bunch of carrots. He placed the greens atop his potato peels and then faced me. "Ellie," he said, "it was a big deal when she left. It would have been a big deal if she came back. But dying is something anybody can do."

"I think being dead is a pretty big deal."

Dad returned to his cutting board. "It would have been good if your mother felt the same way."

"What is that supposed to mean?"

Dad grabbed a chop knife and split a skull-size pumpkin in half with one sharp blow. "It means there's nothing anybody can do about it now."

"We'll see about that."

I said it as if I had some plan to call on my mother's ghost and invite her to a cookout or something. But there's no plan. I just didn't appreciate the fact that Dad shut me down by murdering a gourd.

Back in the stands, the clock is winding down and the Wolves are trying to avoid a shutout. A few rows below me, Mr. DeGroot, our band director, is waving his arms like one of those inflatable flailing tube guys you see in front of used car lots and furniture stores. He's leading us in a marching band version of "Girls Just Want to Have Fun." It's an odd choice to cheer on a football team, but then Mr. DeGroot, who's only been teaching at St. Francis for about a year, is an odd man. Still, the piece is fun to play, and we sound pretty good. Also, it gives me an opportunity to take out some frustration on the glockenspiel, which is sort of like whacking on a set of butter knives attached to a metal frame that hangs over your shoulders. My real instrument is piano, but there's no such thing as a marching piano.

On the field, our quarterback takes a snap, steps back, and heaves a deep pass into the end zone. The ball tumbles over a defender's hands, bounces off at least one St. Francis helmet, and somehow drops into the arms of a very surprised Howling Wolf receiver for the score. There's still no way we're going to win this game, but it's our first touchdown in weeks. From the reaction in the stands, you'd think we just won the Super Bowl. Daniel tilts his head back and howls. *"Arooooooo!"*

The entire St. Francis band responds to Daniel's Wolf Pack call. *"Arooooooo!"*

Encouraged by our classmates' enthusiasm, Daniel shouts, *"JUMP ON IT!"*

"Jump on It" is an old hip-hop tune with an awesome marching band arrangement. It's one of our favorite things to play, and the thought of it makes me smile even though I'm still mad at my father and sad about my mother and honestly sort of confused about everything.

"JUMP ON IT!" Daniel yells again.

Our drum major, Hannah Shupe, glances toward Mr. DeGroot. Hannah started the school year with long red hair, but now she's got a short-cropped pixie cut. Mr. DeGroot just rolls his eyes, so Hannah takes the lead and counts off. "ONE! TWO! THREE! JUMP!"

Our brass section roars to life, the drum line goes crazy, and I start hammering the glockenspiel as if I'm trying to beat it into submission. Meanwhile, the whole band is hopping and waving and dancing because that's what we do for "Jump on It." According to Daniel, St. Francis himself is up in heaven leading a conga line when we play the song. It's really that good.

Approaching the finale, Daniel bounces up and down like a short, skinny pogo stick in a blue-and-gold polyester marching band uniform. On the last note, he takes a big breath, blows into his instrument, and leaps into the air. He hits the high note but turns his ankle on the landing. He gasps, coughs, and spits the piccolo out of his mouth. It flies like an airborne torpedo and ricochets off the side of my head.

"Hey!" I cry.

"Sorry!" Daniel says.

I grab for the piccolo, but it falls to the bleachers, and then drops into the dark space beneath the stands.

"Uh-oh," says Daniel.

He and I stare into the gloom below. "It can't have gone very far," I tell him.

"I hope not."

"Do you want me to help you?"

"It's my fault," Daniel says. "I'll get it." He adjusts his plumed shako, which is tipped so far back it looks like the Leaning Tower of Pisa on his head. Once the feathered hat is straight, he starts limping down the bleachers.

Even without a twisted ankle, Daniel limps everywhere he goes. If you ask, he will explain that he's got "a mild form of monoplegia due to nonspastic dyskinetic cerebral palsy acquired during the prenatal period." In other words, Daniel was born with one foot turned at an angle that makes him walk with a noticeably uneven gait. According to Daniel, the foot issue dashed his Olympic pole-vaulting dreams before they even began. Sometimes he worries that his parents' divorce, which happened before Daniel was a year old, might be a result of the foot issue too. My father promises that it's not. Dad also points out that both Mr. and Mrs. Field were a few fries short of a Happy Meal long before Daniel arrived. Fortunately, Daniel knows that my father never lies. At least not to other people's children.

With the football game almost over, the band begins prepping instruments for our march off the field. Daniel tries to hurry down the small set of bleachers, but before he gets to the bottom, Mr. DeGroot steps into his path. "Where do you think you're going?" the teacher asks.

"I dropped my piccolo," Daniel explains.

"How exactly did that happen?" A sharp-trimmed beard plus shaggy black hair make Mr. DeGroot look like a cross between a comic book villain and an ungroomed poodle.

Daniel glances at his feet. "I just, um, I . . ."

"Spit it out, Mr. Field."

"Actually," says Daniel, "that's how I dropped it."

"Excuse me?"

Daniel grins. "I spit it out."

Mr. DeGroot folds his arms across his chest. "Everything's a joke to you, isn't it?"

Daniel shakes his head. "I never joke about hamsters. Actually, the entire rodent family is off-limits. Mice, rats, gerbils, capybaras, they're all a little shifty if you ask me."

Mr. DeGroot stares at Daniel without speaking.

"Do you know anybody who likes capybaras?" Daniel asks him.

"Go find your piccolo!" Mr. DeGroot is clearly not amused.

"Yes, sir!" Daniel offers a mock salute, then tries to continue down the steps, but he stumbles over his own feet and falls straight into the music teacher's arms. "Oops!" Daniel cries.

Mr. DeGroot struggles to untangle himself from Daniel. "Get off me!"

"Oops!" Daniel says again.

"Is that all you can say?"

"Oopsy-daisy?"

Mr. DeGroot puts Daniel back on his feet with a shove that's more like a punch.

"Hey!" Daniel cries, and nearly falls once more.

Mr. DeGroot reaches out and gives Daniel a second thump on the shoulder.

Daniel regains his feet. "You can't do that!"

"Really?" Mr. DeGroot gives Daniel another tap.

"What if I do the same thing to you?" Daniel suggests.

Mr. DeGroot straightens his jacket and turns to face Daniel. "I wouldn't recommend it."

Daniel is a full head shorter than our teacher, but for as long as I've known him—which is forever—I've never seen Daniel back down from anything. In fact, Daniel is the sort of person who looks for opportunities to not back down. According to him, stubbornness and belligerence are side effects of growing up in an ableist society. Ableism, Daniel explained to me, is what happens when people assume that you're weak, or stupid, or unimportant just because you walk with a limp. Personally, I think the obstinacy, assertiveness, and occasional aggressive tendencies might also be related to being an only child raised by a single parent who can't say the name of their ex-spouse without wanting to commit murder.

Right now, rather than retreat, I'm pretty sure Daniel is going to haul off and punch Mr. DeGroot in the face. Personally, I've always wanted to punch somebody in the face who actually deserves it, and Mr. DeGroot might be the perfect candidate. But I don't know if a dropped piccolo is really worth it. On the other hand, it's always a good day to stick up for a friend.

I glance toward the scoreboard, which shows forty-three seconds left to play. Inscribed above the game clock, the St. Francis of Assisi school motto says: LORD, MAKE ME AN

INSTRUMENT OF YOUR PEACE. I wonder if that's a message from God or just irony.

Either way, I lift the glockenspiel harness over my shoulder, put two hands beneath the instrument, and hurl it forward. The glockenspiel flies about as well as a bag of hammers. It drops quickly, tumbles onto the bleachers, and stops just short of Mr. DeGroot's feet. He hops back, and now it's our teacher's turn to trip, fall, and land atop a few alto saxophones. Meanwhile, the pieces of glock continue cartwheeling down the metal grandstand, jingling and jangling like an ice-cream truck tumbling over a cliff. They come to a stop on the sidelines, where fans and even a few football players gather around the broken remains. A moment later, a final horn announces that the game is over.

I jog down the steps toward Mr. DeGroot, who is tangled in the brass. Daniel stares at me in shock. The rest of the band looks as if I just tossed a hand grenade rather than a musical instrument.

"At least I wasn't playing the piano," I say to nobody in particular.

CHAPTER 2: IN MY OWN DEFENSE

On Saturday morning, Dad and I stand at the St. Francis of Assisi side door entrance. We're waiting for Sister Stephanie Leary, our principal, who instructed us to meet her here. "Do you think this is about the glockenspiel?" I ask.

My father adjusts the blue knit cap that covers his shaved head. "Anybody ever tell you there's no such thing as a dumb question, Ellie?"

"Yes."

"You just proved them wrong."

I stick my tongue out at my father. "I never wanted to play the glockenspiel in the first place."

That's a lie, but I feel like I need to say something in my own defense.

Dad gives a little laugh. "After last night, nobody's going to ask you to play the glockenspiel ever again."

I press my face against a window and try to see into the school building. Nothing's moving in there. Meanwhile, a dim-bulb sun tries to burn through the October gray sky, and a chill breeze presses a pile of dead leaves against the school building. I pull my sleeves down over my hands to keep warm. Halloween is just a few days away. Oddly, an ice-cream truck chimes in the distance.

"I hear your dream car," I tell my father.

Dad rubs his hands together. "I hear the ghost of glockenspiels past."

"Very funny."

Dad is a chef who oversees breakfasts and lunches at Trinity College on the other side of town, but he hopes to run his own fleet of food trucks one day. Basically, he wants to own and operate a chain of gourmet pizza places on wheels. He's even got a name. Pizza Alato!, which means "Winged Pizza!" in Italian. Personally, I think he should call it Magari Pizza because Magari is our last name, but Magari means "Maybe" in Italian, and Dad says he'd prefer something more definite. I think he just likes the idea of a truck decorated with little flying pizzas.

"You could turn an old ice-cream truck into a great pizza bus," I suggest.

"We'll see," Dad says. "Let's get you to college first."

"I'll go to college," I promise.

"Yes," Dad says in a no-nonsense voice. "You will."

Dad works at Trinity College because employee kids get free tuition. I understand that. And I appreciate it. But what if I don't want to go to Trinity? "We should talk about it," I say.

Dad shoves his hands into his pockets. "There's nothing to talk about, Ellie."

Just then, the school door swings open, and Sister Stephanie steps outside. During the week, her outfits are smart and professional. Now she's wearing a baggy, brown sweater, blue jeans, and a pair of worn hiking boots. Plus, she's got her hair pulled back in a loose, gray ponytail. She tilts her head as if she's trying to hear something in the distance. "Ellie Magari," she says to me, "is there an ice-cream truck nearby?"

"He just drove past," I tell her.

"Good," Sister says. "I can never say no to the ice-cream man." She turns away and heads inside. "Follow me."

The side door brings us into the St. Francis gymnasium. The lights are off, but the polished, wood floor reflects a red glow from several illuminated EXIT signs. With Sister Stephanie in the lead, we cut across the basketball court, leave the gym, and head down a hallway that is surprisingly dark. Fortunately, we all know our way around. According to Dad, the place hasn't changed much since he went to school here.

Once upon a time, Sister Stephanie was a St. Francis of Assisi student too. In fact, her yearbook photo hangs right next to Dad's on the Howling Wolves Athletic Wall of Fame. Among other things, Dad earned multiple all-state honors in baseball, basketball, and football. I can't remember Sister Stephanie's sport, but it doesn't surprise me that she was awesome. Before Sister took charge at St. Francis, she was the elementary principal at St. Corentin of Quimper, where Daniel and I and a lot of our friends went to school. At St. Corentin's, Sister Stephanie started a drama club, led the marching band, and established a coed, year-round basketball league. St. Corentin of Quimper is the patron saint of seafood, so Sister also organized monthly fish dinners that brought hundreds of guests and thousands of dollars to our little grade school. It didn't hurt that Dad did most of the cooking.

In the hallway, a bit of gray daylight glows beneath closed classroom doors, so we move out of pitch-black and into dim shadows. I am struck by a sudden thought. "Sister," I say, "did you know my mother?"

"A little," she says without slowing down. "I was a senior when your mom and dad were sophomores."

"My mother died," I say.

The words are strange to say and even stranger to hear. Sister Stephanie must feel the same way, because she stops so quickly that Dad and I nearly crash into her. "I'm so sorry," she says. "I didn't know."

"Thank you," I say, even though I don't know exactly what I'm thanking her for.

Sister glances at my father as if she expects him to say something. He remains silent.

"I remember your mother as a real piece of work," Sister adds.

"In a good way?" I ask.

Sister Stephanie shrugs. "We were kids."

"Ellie never met her," Dad offers. "I haven't seen her in years. Are we going to your office?"

Sister considers my father's response, which is somewhere

between restrained and rude. "Not quite," she finally says. We end up in a nearby classroom, where Sister Stephanie points at a projector hanging from the ceiling. "We're going to need some technology for this."

Dad and I slide into adjacent student desks while Sister Stephanie fusses with a laptop that's propped on a podium. A moment later, a video of the St. Francis Marching Band covers the whiteboard at the front of the room.

"Is that from last night?" I ask.

"It is." Sister Stephanie hits a key on the laptop, and the classroom fills with the "Jump on It" beat, which, I have to say, still sounds great. On the board, Daniel and I are dancing, the band is jumping, and then the piccolo is flying. Now Daniel and Mr. DeGroot have met on the stairs. The tension is rising, and suddenly a glockenspiel soars into view. The camera captures the silver instrument's brief flight as it crashes and careens all the way down to the field. Without warning, the person filming the scene swivels back around and finds our band teacher sprawled on his backside.

"Cut!" Sister Stephanie calls out. She halts the playback.

The classroom is quiet for a long time. Just a couple of feet away, the expression on my father's face reminds me of a time during the summer between first and second grades. Dad and I had walked to a park near our house so I could play on the playground. We stumbled across two middle school boys lying in the grass sharing a cheap BB gun. They were taking turns firing at the crows and grackles that landed on top of the nearby swing set. There were kids playing on that swing set. Dad snatched the gun, snapped it over his knee, and gave each boy a piece of the rifle. One of them opened his mouth to protest. Before he could speak, Dad held out a hand to stop him. "A million years of evolution suggests that it's not always the strong that survive," Dad said. "Sometimes it's the silent."

The boys ran home. Silently. Right now, I'm thinking it would be good for me to be as quiet as possible too.

"I can't believe you threw that glockenspiel," Dad finally says to me.

I shrug. "It seemed like the right thing to do at that time." So much for silence.

Neither Dad nor Sister offers a reply.

"It might have been the highlight of the game," I add.

"You should know that I've fired Mr. DeGroot," Sister Stephanie announces.

Dad's head whips around as fast as mine.

"I have high expectations for every member of the St. Francis school community," she continues. "Mr. DeGroot did not meet those expectations."

"You fired him?" I say.

"I fired him," Sister tells me, "and now we're moving on."

Dad considers the small woman at the front of the room. "You haven't changed much, have you?" he asks.

"In some ways yes," says Sister. "In some ways no."

Dad turns to me. "Sister Stephanie ran cross-country in high school."

"That's true," she says. "I also played tuba in the marching band."

"Is that why your picture's on the Wall of Fame?" I ask.

Sister shares a quick smile. "It wasn't for the tuba."

"She was Cross-Country State Champion four years in a row," Dad tells me. "And that's a sport that requires speed, endurance, and a very high tolerance for pain."

Sister shrugs. "It was a good way to see if I had what it takes to be a Catholic school principal."

"You used to wear a T-shirt," Dad continues. "It said—"

Sister finishes the sentence. "Somebody may beat me, but they are going to have to bleed to do it."

"Too bad Mr. DeGroot never saw that shirt," says Dad.

"He saw it," Sister replies. "It's hanging in my office right now."

"You had it in your office at St. Corentin's too," I recall. "It was right next to a poster that said, 'It's a bird. It's a plane. It's the flying nun.'"

Sister grins a little. "I love the flying nun."

The flying nun poster showed a smiling, dark-haired girl wearing a long, white religious habit and a huge, pale headpiece shaped like a pair of wings. Apparently, the hat enabled her to soar above the seaside towns pictured below her feet. When I was little, I assumed the picture was young Sister Stephanie leaving the convent for the very first time. Even now, it wouldn't surprise me to learn that I was right.

"With luck, Mr. DeGroot will be the last person to see my decorations and believe that they're only there for decoration." Sister points at the image frozen on the wall. "Speaking of Mr. DeGroot, this video does not capture exactly how the man ended on top of his alto sax section." She turns to me. "What happened?"

"Did Daniel punch the guy?" Dad asks.

I shake my head. "It was my fault."

"You punched him?" says Sister.

"No. He jumped back and tripped after I threw the glockenspiel."

Dad runs a hand over his head. "Did you really have to throw the thing?"

"Did you really have to tell me my mother was dead just before I headed off to the football game?"

"Wait a minute," says Sister. "When did she die?"

"A couple weeks ago," says Dad.

"A couple weeks ago?" This is news to me. "You didn't tell me till yesterday!"

"I wouldn't have told you at all, but then I thought her obituary might show up in the *Rockhill Free Press*."

"Did it?" asks Sister Stephanie.

Dad shakes his head. "Korky moved to Boston years ago. There's no reason for her to show up in the Rockhill newspaper now, but you never know." He turns to me. "I thought it would be better if you heard it from me."

"Gee," I say, "thanks."

"Ellie," says Dad. "You never even met her. Stop talking like this is some kind of—"

"It just would have been nice to meet her one day," I continue. "Now that's never going to happen."

"Guess what," says Dad. "There's lots of things that are never going to happen. You'll never take a piano lesson from Beethoven. I'll never pitch for the Red Sox. Neither one of us is going to steal the Millennium Falcon and destroy the Death Star."

Dad and I are both huge Star Wars fans.

"Bruce," Sister Stephanie says to my father. "You are intentionally missing the point."

"Here's the point," says Dad. "There are seven billion people on the planet. Ellie won't meet most of them, and she'll be just fine."

I cross my arms. "Only one of those seven billion strangers was my mother. In case you can't pick her out, she's stacked with the dead ones."

My father gets to his feet.

"Sit down!" Sister yells at him.

Surprisingly, Dad sits.

Sister turns to me. "Ellie, is this why you tossed a thousand-dollar musical instrument down the grandstand?"

"It probably influenced my decision," I admit.

Sister Stephanie sighs. "It seems that you and Mr. DeGroot both carried some baggage into that football game."

"I have a dead mom," I say. "What's his excuse?"

"I'm not sure that it's any of your business," the principal snaps at me.

"Sorry," I mumble.

"Apology accepted." Sister Stephanie points at the image of Mr. DeGroot still tangled in the saxophonists on the board. "Now please tell me how we got to this."

I take a big breath and try to explain. "We were just playing and dancing, and then the piccolo hit me in the back of the head. That was an accident. Daniel was going to get it, and suddenly Mr. DeGroot was being a bully."

"That's when you stepped in?" says Sister.

"Daniel has a temper," I say. "I didn't want him to do something stupid."

"Thank goodness you were there to save the day," says Dad.

"Bruce," Sister says in a forced calm voice, "sarcasm is rarely an effective parenting technique."

"Rarely," Dad says. "But not never."

The principal turns back to me. "Go on."

"I was already angry because of everything else. It felt like the whole world was going crazy. I just wanted it to stop."

Sister Stephanie nods. "I know the feeling well."

"Do you deal with it by tossing a glockenspiel?" Dad asks her.

"It's not an option I'd ever considered," she admits.

"It worked for me," I say.

"Unfortunately not so much for me." Sister Stephanie leans against a desk. "Thanks to your flying glockenspiel, I have to meet with the superintendent, the school board, and my staff to let them know that I fired a teacher because of inappropriate conduct. I'll have to make some kind of announcement to parents and students too. I'll probably get a call from a newspaper reporter because there is an online video that appears to show a St. Francis of Assisi faculty member bullying one kid while another kid tosses a very expensive musical instrument down a flight of bleacher stairs. Meanwhile, the same video suggests that a member of our marching band may have assaulted an adult, who, quite frankly, might have deserved it."

Dad opens his mouth as if he's about to speak.

"Wait," says Sister Stephanie, "there's more. I'll have to explain all this to our teachers' union. I have to find a new music instructor. I need to purchase a new glockenspiel. Most importantly, I have to make sure that all our students take away an appropriate lesson from this fiasco."

"And a piccolo," I say.

"What?" says Sister.

"Daniel and I never found the piccolo."

Sister Stephanie's eyes narrow.

"But we'll go back and look again," I add quickly.

"Good," she says. "You're also going to do a billion hours of community service, and I'm going to announce that you've agreed to pay for the glockenspiel."

"Wait a minute," says Dad. "A thousand dollars—"

"Don't worry," Sister tells him. "The school insurance will cover the cost of the instrument, but a principal should never miss an opportunity to appear unreasonably harsh."

Dad relaxes a bit. "Okay. That makes sense."

"No, it doesn't," I say.

"Nobody asked you," Dad tells me.

"Can I say something?" I ask.

"You can say thank you," says Dad.

"For what?"

"For not getting suspended, expelled, or charged with assault and battery."

"But I did the right thing!" I protest. "Why am I getting punished?"

"Ellie," says Sister Stephanie, "why did you ever think that doing the right thing would cost nothing?"

CHAPTER 3: THE SQUARE ROOT OF 29,584

On Sunday, Daniel and I wade through small piles of wind-blown trash while we look for his piccolo beneath the Howling Wolf bleachers. Nearby, a metal trash can tipped on its side explains the mess. Raccoons must have knocked the bin over during the night. I step over limp French fries and red, plastic cups that hold nothing but the syrupy, sweet smell of old, flat soda. On the plus side, I'm finding a lot of loose change.

Daniel spots a stick in the dirt. He grabs it and uses it to sweep garbage out of his way.

I find two more dimes and a quarter to add to my pocket. "I really think Sister Stephanie has a crush on my father."

"You've mentioned that about a thousand times." Daniel ducks to avoid smacking his head on a low-hanging metal beam. "First of all, she doesn't. Second of all, so what?"

"So she's a nun." I nudge an empty popcorn box with my toe in the hopes that it's hiding a piccolo. It's not.

"She wasn't always a nun," Daniel reminds me.

"I think she still likes him."

"Everybody likes your dad, Ellie."

"I don't," I say.

"That's because you're not a nun with a secret crush."

I tip over another sticky cup. "Not funny, Daniel."

He continues swinging the stick through the trash. "Imagine if Sister Stephanie was your mom."

"Shut up." I told Daniel about my dead mom earlier in the day. He knows she's been missing for years. News that she's dead is a new wrinkle.

"Having a nun for a mother would probably be complicated," he suggests.

"What part of shut up do you not understand?"

"That would be all the parts." He pokes at a couple of old football programs while the last sunshine of the day filters through the metal bleachers above us.

"Just find the piccolo, okay?"

He stops. "It's not my fault that we're down here, Ellie."

"Actually," I tell him, "it is."

Daniel considers this. "Okay," he finally says. "That's true, but—"

"But nothing. You dropped the piccolo. I'm the one with a billion hours of community service. Besides that, I'm supposed to figure out who posted the online video and convince them to take it down."

Daniel holds up his hand, then waves a finger in the air as if he's working out a math problem on an invisible chalkboard. "According to my calculations," he tells me, "it will take approximately one hundred and fourteen thousand years to finish a billion hours of community service." He lowers his hand. "I can see why you're upset."

"I'm not upset." I give a green, plastic soda bottle a ferocious kick. The empty container ricochets off a rusty electrical box and nearly hits Daniel in the head.

"I'm glad you're not upset," he says.

"Maybe I'm a little upset."

"Would you feel better if we found your mom?" Daniel asks.

"I'd feel better if we found the piccolo."

Daniel lifts his stick and points at a knothole in the wooden bench directly above my head. "I was sitting right there."

I lean back, look around, and spot the shiny, silver instrument just an arm's length away. It's balanced on an old metal beam, so I reach up, grab the thing, and hand it to Daniel. He drops the stick, takes the piccolo, and begins to play "Yankee Doodle Dandy" while we head out from beneath the bleachers and back toward open sky.

"Hey, Pied Piper," I say. "Let's go home."

Daniel lowers his piccolo. "The Pied Piper was a medieval German rat catcher, Ellie. You know how I feel about rodents."

Just then, I notice a figure walking toward the end zone near the school parking lot. "Speaking of rodents."

Daniel turns to see what I'm looking at. "Is that Mr. DeGroot?"

Even at this distance, the beard and the shaggy hair make it easy to identify our former band teacher. "That's him," I say.

"What's he doing?"

I squint. "It looks like he's coming our way."

Daniel says nothing.

I take his arm. "Let's get out of here."

"I'm not afraid of him," Daniel tells me.

"He lost his job because of us."

"He lost his job because of himself."

"He might not see it that way," I point out.

"Then he's seeing it wrong."

"I still don't want to talk to him." Above us, the sky is turning from a late afternoon coral pink into deep evening purple and blue. I pull Daniel toward the path that cuts through the nearby woods and leads back to our neighborhood. "Let's leave Mr. DeGroot alone."

Daniel follows, but he doesn't look away from the man on the other side of the field.

"Do you want to have supper at my house tonight?" I ask as we make our way toward home.

Daniel shoves his piccolo into a coat pocket. "Is one hundred and seventy-two the square root of twenty-nine thousand five hundred and eighty-four?"

"I have no idea."

"It is," says Daniel. "And after supper, we can visit Anya Flowers."

Anya Flowers is a tall, dark-haired, Asian girl who attended seventh and eighth grades at St. Corentin's with Daniel and me. Now she's a St. Francis of Assisi freshman just like us. I never spent much time with Anya when we were at St. Corentin's. I still don't hang out with her. It's not that I dislike her. It's just that she's in all honors classes. I am not. Also, Anya's sort of supermodel pretty, which is one more thing that I am not.

"Why would we visit Anya Flowers?"

"Because Anya is the one who took the video last night."

"When were you going to mention that?"

Daniel pulls out his phone and checks the time. "At exactly seventeen minutes past five o'clock." He looks up and grins. "I'm right on time."

CHAPTER 4: DEAD MOM IN A SHOE BOX

Daniel's father runs the service department for Rockhill Automotive. His mom works in the produce section at the Rockhill Market. I'd like to say that they're both very nice people, but honestly, Mr. Field is a grouchy, pear-shaped man who rarely visits his son. Daniel's mother is a small, raspy-voiced woman who likes to garden but hates to cook. She's usually tired and cranky from working most of the time. In any case, Daniel eats with me and Dad almost every night. Daniel's fascinated by the whole culinary thing, so he generally helps Dad with the cooking too.

"We're home!" Daniel calls when we step into my kitchen.

Dad's usually mixing up corn biscuits or sautéing vegetables or maybe even baking a cake by now. Tonight, there's nothing.

"Hello?" I say.

"The chef doesn't seem to be in," Daniel observes.

"Dad?" I holler.

"In here." My father's voice comes from the living room, where we find him sitting on the sofa. A plain, fat shoe box rests at his feet.

"What are you doing?" I ask when we enter the room.

"I'm thinking."

I pull my sweatshirt over my head. "About what?"

"About how much I enjoy hearing you play the piano." He points at our old upright on the opposite side of the room. It's a massive, mahogany monster that looks like a stack of dark coffins with a keyboard attached to the front. "How about a song?"

"I'm still mad at you," I tell him.

"One song?" Dad says.

Daniel plops onto the sofa beside my father. "Come on, Ellie."

"Fine." I cross the room, toss my sweatshirt on the piano

bench, and take a seat facing the keyboard. Without comment, I begin a Beethoven piece that Dad's heard a million times.

"Can't you play something I like?" he asks.

I stop playing and stare at a worn, metal emblem screwed above the keyboard. The label identifies the piano as a LESTER CABINET GRAND. I turn toward my father. "Lester wants Beethoven."

"Lester doesn't pay for your lessons."

"Fine," I say again. I improvise a bluesy, eight-to-the-bar number that, I have to admit, sounds great because Lester is more honky-tonk riffraff than concert hall diva. When I finish, I spin around on the bench and face the sofa. "Ta-da."

"Thank you," says Dad. "In exchange, I will now share something with you." He lifts the shoe box off the floor.

"What's in the box?" asks Daniel.

"Ellie's mother," Dad says simply.

Daniel scoots to the other end of the couch.

"Relax," Dad says. "She's not actually in the box."

Daniel still looks nervous.

"She hasn't been in this house for a very long time," Dad adds.

"What are you talking about?" I ask.

Dad drums his fingers on the lid of the box. "There's stuff in here for you."

"What kind of stuff?" I ask.

"Photos, postcards, assorted junk."

"From my mother?"

Dad leans forward and gives me the box.

Daniel slides back toward the middle of the sofa. "Did she leave all this for Ellie in her will or something?"

"I don't know about any will," says Dad. "The box arrived a little over a year ago. I assume that Korky sent it."

I look up at my father. "You've had this for over a year?"

"She wasn't supposed to send you anything," Dad tells me. "She was supposed to come and talk to you herself. Your mother and I had a deal."

"What kind of deal?"

Dad stands and paces the room. "When Korky left, I made her promise that she would not be sending you millions of little cards and presents and toys."

"What's wrong with cards and presents and toys?" Daniel asks.

"Ellie would have grown up thinking one of her parents was some kind of magic gift-giving angel, and the other one was me." Dad shakes his head. "I wasn't going to let that happen."

"Congratulations," I say. "Goal achieved."

Dad stops pacing, then sits beside me on the piano bench. "If Korky wanted to say something, she was supposed to come back and say it in person."

"That was the deal?" I say.

"Did she ever come back?" asks Daniel.

"Yes, that was the deal," Dad says. "No, she never came back."

I consider the shoe box. "Apparently, she still had something to say."

"I think she wanted you to know about her band," Dad tells me.

"What band?" I give the box a little shake. "What else is in here?"

"Compact discs," says Dad. "A few cassettes."

"You already opened it?" I ask.

"I didn't trust her," Dad confesses.

"What could she send in a shoe box?" I ask.

"Scorpions," says Daniel. "Fire ants. Poison dart frogs." He gives an involuntary shudder. "Naked mole rats."

Dad says nothing, but he probably had similar thoughts, so I decide to let it go. "What did you say about a band?" I ask.

"Korky always dreamt of being in a rock and roll band," Dad explains. "Apparently, her dream came true."

"Ellie's mom was a rock star?" Daniel's eyes go wide.

Dad shakes his head. "That's not what I said."

Daniel points at the box in my hands. "Open it!"

I slide off the piano bench and onto the floor in front of the couch. Daniel sits with me on the carpet. Slowly, I lift the lid off the shoe box. Inside, a balled-up leopard-print scarf and a pair of dark, cat-eye sunglasses sit atop a bunch of plastic cassette tapes and shiny CDs.

"Except for a few souvenirs," says Dad, "it's mostly music."

I grab the discs and tapes and hand them to Daniel. He reads the names of strange bands and unfamiliar singers out loud. "The Bangles. Cyndi Lauper. Martha and the Muffins."

I look up at my dad. "Martha and the Muffins?"

He shrugs. "Cyndi Lauper was her favorite."

"Kirsty MacColl," Daniel continues. "Haysi Fantayzee, Curiosity Killed the Cat, Kajagoogoo, THE Jam."

I pull another CD out of the box. "This one's from a group called Men without Hats. What happened to their hats?"

Daniel holds up a tape labeled A FLOCK OF SEAGULLS. "Maybe a flock of seagulls took them?"

"That's all music from the 1980s," Dad explains. "Korky loved that stuff. She must have wanted to share it with you."

"Why?" I ask.

"People like to share things with their kids, Ellie."

"My mother has been gone for my whole life, and now I get a year-old shoe box two weeks after she's dead. You call this sharing?"

"I didn't force her to stay away," Dad tells me. "She did that herself."

I point at the music collection that Daniel and I have spread out on the floor. "It looks like she was trying to come back."

"By sending Men without Hats?" Dad asks, clearly annoyed.

"Seriously," says Daniel. "What happened to their hats?"

"Nobody cares about the hats!" Dad and I snap at the same time.

From the tone of Dad's voice, I suddenly understand that my father might still have feelings for this woman I've never even met. I suppose I should feel some sympathy for his loss. Instead, I feel like I've stuck my hand on a live wire, and I can't let go. "I think that my mother would have liked to meet me," I inform my dad. "I think I would have liked to have known her. Thanks to you, that's never going to happen."

Dad stands and puts a hand on the piano top, which holds assorted photos and keepsakes, including a fat glass fish attached to a plaque that says BRUCE MAGARI AND ST. CORENTIN OF QUIMPER, OUR PATRON SAINTS OF SEA-FOOD. It strikes me that none of this stuff suggests that I ever even had a mom. I could have been cloned.

"Ellie," Dad says, "if it was up to me, she would have never left."

"That's nice, but it doesn't make her any less gone." I get to my feet and grab my sweatshirt. "Daniel and I have to go out," I announce.

"We do?" says Daniel.

I kneel down to gather everything off the carpet and shove it back into the shoe box. "We're going to see Anya Flowers."

Daniel glances between Dad and me. "When?"

I stand, pull out my phone, and check the time. "At exactly nineteen minutes past six o'clock, and guess what." I head for the door. "We're right on time."

CHAPTER 5: *CYNDI LAUPER'S NOT DEAD!*

Daniel catches up with me across the street. I'm sitting on the back bumper of his mother's old hatchback with a shoe box in my lap and a sweatshirt over my arm. Daniel leans against a rusty fender. "It's cold out," he says. "Put your sweatshirt on."

"It's not my sweatshirt." It's true. My father gets shirts out of the lost-and-found box at Trinity College's cafeteria. This one features the school's mascot, a phoenix, which represents beauty, luck, resurrection, and Harry Potter.

"Just put it on," Daniel tells me.

I pull the thing over my head. "Can we visit Anya Flowers now?"

"Do you even know where she lives?"

"No idea," I admit.

Daniel sighs. "Follow me." He stands, steadies himself against the side of the car, then walks up his driveway and toward the garage door that's stuck halfway down.

Watching Daniel walk away, it appears that he's favoring his leg more than usual. "Are you okay?" I ask.

"My ankle's sore from falling down the bleachers," he admits.

His leg must really hurt, because Daniel hates to let anything slow him down. Seriously, if he impaled himself on a Viking sword, he'd go for a bike ride, shop for groceries, then help Dad dig a barbecue pit before he asked for a Band-Aid.

I remain at the end of the driveway and stare at Daniel until he finally turns around.

"Really," he says before I can speak again. "I'm fine." Daniel tries to duck beneath the half-open garage door. Rather than slip into the garage, he smacks his head on the door's bottom rail. "I meant to do that."

"Nice job, then."

At school, our friends think Daniel and I get along like an old married couple. While it's true that I love Daniel very much, it's also true that I know exactly what it's like to live with a stubborn mule. In other words, being married to Daniel would be like living with my father for the rest of my life. I don't see that happening.

I tuck my shoe box under one arm and follow Daniel. Inside the garage, we maneuver past a couple of rusty lawn mowers, an old charcoal grill, and three or four snow shovels, including one that has a picture of Mickey Mouse on the blade. Daniel leads us to the garage's back door, which opens into his yard covered in autumn-brown grass and papery, dry leaves.

"Where are we going?" I ask.

Daniel points across Rockhill Memorial Cemetery, which runs alongside all the backyards on this side of our street. "Anya lives on the other side of the graveyard."

I consider the cemetery, currently bathed in a waist-high mist and an orange, ghostly glow from the fat, October moon rising in the east. "You seriously want me to hike across an ancient burial ground beneath a full moon just a few days before Halloween and a few days after I inherited a dead mom?"

"The moon's not full, the cemetery's not that old, and more people are attacked by squirrels than by dead people." Daniel turns and heads toward the graveyard. "There's no need to worry. Most of the squirrels are already hibernating."

I lift the shoe box. "What about this?"

Daniel glances back over his shoulder. "Leave it in the garage."

I duck back into the garage, shove my carton behind the Mickey Mouse shovel, then turn and catch up with Daniel.

Maybe Daniel's leg really doesn't hurt that badly because he and I practically sprint through the mist and across the cemetery. Soon, we're walking past tall, fancy houses and redbrick mansions that have things like cupolas and porches and roofs made out of slate. It's hard to believe that the only thing separating our neighborhood from this one is a small field filled with grave markers and dead people.

I glance at a gigantic home decked out with hundreds of tiny carved pumpkins, several well-dressed scarecrows, and a complicated Halloween lighting display that includes spooky music, orange lasers, and a fog machine. Those decorations probably cost more than Dad would need to buy his first pizza truck.

Daniel stops in front of a tidy, green cottage-style home with a couple of lit jack-o'-lanterns on either side of the front door. "I think this is it," he tells me.

"You think? You're not sure?"

Daniel takes out his phone and pokes at the screen for a moment. "I'm sure."

"How do you know?"

"Pickler's intuition."

"What's a pickler?" I ask.

"It's what you call a piccolo player."

"No," I say. "It's not."

Daniel rolls his eyes. "As if a glockler would know."

"Has anybody mentioned that you're annoying?" I ask him.

He gives me a grin. "I don't recall it ever coming up."

Together, we approach the cottage's front door, which is set beneath a wide, white archway. Long panes of beautiful stained glass featuring painted mermaids and tropical fish cover the top half of the door. A fat, silver doorknob shaped like a seashell completes the effect. I point at a bunch of tiny white stones set into the granite pavers at our feet. The stones spell out a phrase. *Witamy w Cyrku*. "What do you think that means?" I ask.

"It's Tibetan," Daniel says confidently.

I know he's lying. "Really?"

He nods. "It says 'Daniel is not annoying.'" He pushes the doorbell button, and a cascade of chimes and chords worthy of the London Symphony Orchestra echoes from inside the house.

"Do you think Anya is rich?" I ask.

"I've never really thought about it," says Daniel.

"News flash," I say. "She's rich."

Before Daniel can reply, Anya Flowers opens the door. She's wearing an oversize, pink sweatshirt over a pair of black leggings. She's even taller and prettier than I remember. "That was fast," she says to Daniel.

"What was fast?" I ask.

Anya turns to me. "Daniel texted to say you were coming over."

"When did he do that?" I ask.

"About five seconds ago."

Daniel shrugs. "I don't like to drop in unannounced."

I point at the letters around our feet. "Is that Tibetan?"

Anya looks down and laughs. "It's Polish. It means 'Welcome to the Circus.'"

"It looks Tibetan," says Daniel.

"I was born in the Sichuan province of China," says Anya. "Sichuan borders Tibet, but my family is part Polish. I'm adopted."

I don't know if there is a correct response to this information. "Congratulations?"

Anya laughs again. "Come in."

We follow her into a high-ceilinged living room where a baby grand piano sits in front of a fieldstone fireplace. Books and paintings and expensive-looking knickknacks fill built-in shelves that surround us. At the same time, photos and old magazines and framed preschool artwork make the room feel homey and comfortable. A finger painting propped in the center of the mantel shows a little girl holding hands with two stick-figure adults. "Is that you?" I ask.

Anya looks embarrassed. "I made that in kindergarten. My parents save everything."

We continue to the kitchen, where a slender African American man and a round-faced white woman sit shoulder to shoulder staring at a million-piece puzzle spread across a large, wooden table. "These are my parents," Anya says.

Daniel reaches out to shake hands with Anya's father. "I've never met anybody from Poland before."

Mrs. Flowers has a big laugh just like Anya's.

"What's so funny?" asks Anya's dad. "It's possible."

"But not likely." Mrs. Flowers has wide, round cheeks, a very light complexion, and a noticeable Eastern European accent. "Most Polish people look more like me than Dr. Flowers," she explains.

"She means because he's black," says Anya.

"I bet they could figure that out," suggests Dr. Flowers.

"This is Daniel and Ellie," Anya tells her parents. "Can we hang out in my room?"

Her mom sighs. "That room is a disaster."

"I'm sure it's not that bad," I say.

"It's pretty bad," says Anya.

"Enter at your own risk," Dr. Flowers tells us.

A moment later, we're in the middle of clothes and books and piles of papers. Several lamps, reading lights, assorted cables, and a laptop computer sit balanced on top of a desk near a dark green wall. Movie posters for *The Life of Pi*, *Because of Winn-Dixie*, and something called *In the Realms of the Unreal* hang above a bed that's buried beneath magazines and notecards.

"This room really is a disaster," Daniel observes.

Anya shoves stuff aside so Daniel and I can sit on the bed. "It only seems disorganized. I know where everything is."

"Ellie wants to ask you about last night's football game," Daniel tells her.

Anya's eyes go wide. "That was wild. But you were awesome," she says to me. "I really thought Mr. DeGroot was going to kill Daniel. And then you threw that thing."

"The glockenspiel," I say.

"Did you get in trouble?"

I nod. "Apparently, there's a rule about throwing musical instruments at teachers."

"It's a sin to kill a glockenspiel," says Daniel.

"I didn't kill it," I tell him.

Daniel raises an eyebrow. "It looked dead to me."

"I caught the whole thing on video," says Anya.

"That's why we're here," I explain. "Sister Stephanie showed the video to my father and me this morning."

Anya looks confused. "How did Sister Stephanie get my video?"

"She got the link somehow," I say. "It caused a big commotion. Mr. DeGroot got fired."

Anya takes a step back. "Wow."

"He deserved it," says Daniel.

"Sister Stephanie hopes you'll take the video down," I tell Anya.

"I can do that." She grabs her laptop, sits on a pile of laundry, then punches a few keys. "There, it's gone."

"You deleted it?" I ask.

She shakes her head. "I just marked it private, so now I'm the only one who can get to the file."

"Why were you taking video, anyway?"

Anya gestures at the computer on her lap and the equipment all around us. "I make movies."

I look around, and Anya's room starts to make a little more sense. It's basically her own personal, Hollywood studio. Besides schoolwork, science fiction novels, a couple of American Girl dolls, plus a complete set of Wizard of Oz books, her shelves are filled with script-writing guides and filmmaking textbooks. Two spindly tripods, a long microphone stand, and several silver battery packs are strewn here and there. Pushpins hold index cards and long pieces of paper to the walls above the bed. Leaning closer, I see that the papers contain stick-figure drawings along with ideas for shots and scenes and dialogue.

"Those are my storyboards," says Anya.

"What's a storyboard?" I ask.

"They're sort of like comic strips," Anya explains. "Story-boards are how you turn words into pictures. Putting a set of pictures into the right order makes a scene, and organizing scenes is how you figure out your story. Once that's done, the storyboard is your plan for shooting the movie."

Daniel pulls a red high-top sneaker from beneath the pillow he's leaning against. "Ellie's trying to figure out a story," he says.

Anya takes the sneaker, reaches inside, and retrieves a plastic baggie filled with rainbow-colored gummy bears. "Do you want to make a movie?"

I shake my head. "No."

"She's searching for clues about her dead mom," Daniel explains.

"When did she die?" Anya asks.

"I don't know exactly," I admit. "It was a couple weeks ago. I never really knew her. I don't know much about her at all."

Anya hands me a gummy bear. "It's weird, isn't it? I don't know anything about my biological mother either. Did you ever look her up online?"

Over the years, I'd considered doing an Internet search. It would be easy enough, and with a name like Korkenderfer, the odds are good that I would find something. But between Dad's information blackout and my own superstition that

I might jinx some possibility of meeting her one day, putting Wilma Korkenderfer into Google always felt like the wrong thing to do. "I never looked," I admit.

Anya places her hands on the laptop keyboard. "May I?"

I take a big breath, then let it out. "Okay," I say mostly to myself. "Her name was Wilma Korkenderfer. Some people called her Korky."

Anya types quickly, then hits ENTER. A second later, a confused look crosses her face. "Why am I looking at Cyndi Lauper?" she asks.

"Cyndi Lauper was her favorite singer," Daniel offers.

Anya's eyes narrow. "Was your mom a singer too?"

"Maybe," I say. "I know she was in a band."

"I think we found her."

Daniel and I slide to the end of the bed so we can see the screen. Anya points at a neon-themed homepage. "Wilma 'Korky' Korkenderfer was the lead singer in a band called *CYNDI LAUPER'S NOT DEAD!*"

"Does Cyndi Lauper know about this?" asks Daniel.

Anya clicks on a new link. When the page opens, it features a full framed photograph of a smiling woman in bright red lipstick, bold green eye shadow, and long, dark hair teased into a shape that is wild and enormous. She's wearing a zebra-print jacket over a neon-green top the same color as a pair of massive rectangular earrings that nearly touch her shoulders.

"That's got to be your mother," Daniel says to me. "She looks just like you!"

I examine the photo closely. "Really?"

"She's very pretty," says Anya.

"She's something," I say.

Anya points at the screen. "According to this, Wilma 'Korky' Korkenderfer died on Tuesday, October 7, following a long, hard battle with leukemia. She formed *CYNDI LAUPER'S NOT DEAD!* more than a decade ago with drummer Seamus Brady, who was also her husband and high school sweetheart. She is dearly missed, and the band continues to be inspired by her passion and her love."

"The band continues?" I say. "Where? When? And who is Seamus Brady?"

Daniel leans forward to see the computer. "Ellie, didn't your mom and dad meet in high school?"

"They did more than meet. My mother was pregnant at their high school graduation." Dad's never pointed this out, but I know it's true because math.

Anya clicks to another page, then zooms in on a dark-haired man holding a pair of drumsticks. "That's Seamus."

"You weren't her only sweetheart, Seamus," Daniel says to the screen.

"Is there anything else?" I ask.

Anya clicks around the site. "It looks like they only play music from the 1980s. They're popular too. They've got at least a couple shows a week all year long. They're even busier in the summer."

"Is there anything else about my mom?" I ask.

"Not that I noticed," says Anya.

"Is there anything in there about Ellie?" says Daniel.

Anya shakes her head. "I don't think anything like that would be on the CYNDI LAUPER'S NOT DEAD! website."

Of course Anya's right. But still, it would be nice to find even the smallest bit of proof that Wilma "Korky" Korkenderfer knew I existed.

"You've still got the shoe box," Daniel reminds me as if he can read my mind.

"What shoe box?" says Anya.

Quickly, we tell her all about the unexpected treasure chest Dad dropped into my lap earlier in the evening.

"How do you know if it's really from your mom?"

"I don't know," I say. "I don't know anything. That's the problem."

"You've got lot of scenes but no story," Anya says thoughtfully.

"You think we should make a storyboard?" says Daniel.

Anya shrugs. "This isn't a movie."

I study the photos scrolling across the screen. Even though Wilma Korkenderfer is gone, it's clear that the band is still alive and kicking. "I have a better idea," I say. Anya's laptop has a touchscreen, so I reach over and put my finger on the link that says SHOWS. A simple calendar appears on the screen, so I scroll down the page. It only takes a moment to find exactly what I am hoping for. *CYNDI LAUPER'S NOT DEAD!* is playing at Trinity College in two weeks.

"Anybody want to go to a show?" I ask.

CHAPTER 6: ROADKILL PIZZA, DANCING FIRECRACKERS, AND A SCORPION IN YOUR POCKET

When I get home, I find my father flipping through bills and paperwork at the kitchen table. A few sad-looking pieces of pizza sit on a plate in front of him. "Are you hungry?" he asks.

I place the cardboard box, which I retrieved from Daniel's garage, on the counter. I point at the pizza slices. "Those look like roadkill."

"I ordered out," Dad admits.

"It definitely doesn't look like something you'd make."

"Eat it or don't," Dad says. "It's up to you."

I pull out a chair and sit. "I had cookies at Anya's."

"Store-bought or homemade?"

"Anya gave us Polish cookies that she made with her mom."

Dad pokes at a limp piece of pizza. "They were probably better for you than this."

"Anya and her mom bake a lot." I hesitate, then ask, "Did my mother bake?"

Dad turns back to the bills. "Korky did not bake."

I wait, but he doesn't add anything else.

I'd intended to come home and take everything I just learned about Wilma "Korky" Korkenderfer and throw it in Dad's face, but if he can keep secrets, so can I. "I'm sorry I stormed out earlier," I offer.

Dad stands and brings the plate of pizza from the table to the garbage. "You were with Daniel. I knew you'd be okay."

For some reason, this makes me angry. I mean, what was the point of storming out in the first place if Dad's not even upset about it? I push myself away from the table and pick up my shoe box. "I'm going to finish my homework."

Dad turns to face me. "You went out and you still had homework?"

"Now you're upset?" I say. "Because I have homework?"

"You know the rules, Ellie. School comes first."

"School comes before a dead mother?"

Dad slaps the kitchen counter so hard that coffee cups rattle inside the cabinets. "Stop talking like she was actually your mother."

"Did she give birth to me or not?"

"You know what I mean."

"So you're saying that I don't have a mother."

"Yes," says Dad. "That is exactly what I'm saying."

"Thanks for clearing that up." I stand, tuck the cardboard treasure chest under my arm, and head for the door.

The next morning, Dad is out of the house before I'm even awake. As usual, he's left a homemade muffin and a glass of fresh orange juice for my breakfast. He's also packed me a brown-bag lunch. Dad's lunches are so good that it's not uncommon for kids to offer me money for them. This morning, I eat a Hershey bar and throw everything else away.

Outside, I meet Daniel on the sidewalk, and we walk to school together like always. Apparently, the world is going to just keep turning despite the fact that my life has been turned upside down. "You're sure we're not suspended or expelled or something?" Daniel asks me.

"I'm sure."

At school, Daniel and I head down the long hallway that runs behind the auditorium and leads to the music room. If you're in the band at St. Francis, you start every day in the music room. The location protects the rest of the building from the honks and screeches and various painful noises we tend to make when we're learning a new piece. Sometimes we make those noises just because we can. In any case, keeping the band away from the quieter parts of teaching and learning is a good idea. This Monday morning, however, there's nothing but silence in the music room. Even our percussion section, typically a collection of hyperactive twitches and finger tapping, is still. Sister Stephanie stands at the desk that used to belong to Mr. DeGroot.

"Here's the thing," Sister announces once the first-period bell stops ringing. "Your old band teacher is no longer a member of the St. Francis High School community."

"What do you mean?" asks a skinny Irish kid we all call Sinbad. His real name, spelled Cinead, is a Gaelic word that every single teacher pronounced incorrectly on the first day of school. "It's Kinny," he tried to tell them.

Not anymore.

"I mean that I have invited Mr. DeGroot to pursue other opportunities," Sister says.

"You canned him?" says Sinbad, who can make a snare drum sound like a collection of dancing firecrackers.

Sister nods. "Pretty much."

Hannah Shupe raises her hand. "What's going to happen to the band? Who's going to be our teacher?"

Josh Rios, who is a six-foot-three-inch sousaphone player as well as a defensive lineman and a heavyweight wrestler, steps forward. "I could do it," he says.

"Just because you're big doesn't mean you should be in charge," says Charlotte Rios, Josh's twin sister, who sits right in front of me.

"Why don't we wrestle for it?" Josh suggests.

"Because I would destroy you," Charlotte tells him.

The class laughs because Josh weighs nearly three hundred pounds, and Charlotte is the size of a stuffed rabbit. Of course, Charlotte marches our field show carrying a quad rack of tenor drums that are twice her size. Every once in a while, she drops the drumsticks and bangs on the drums by hand, which compels Josh to begin a Puerto Rican bomba dance that looks like a cross between running in place with a scorpion in your pocket and hugging a pack of invisible puppies. Now that I think of it, I feel like I've been doing the bomba for several days now. In any case, if it comes to a wrestling match, I'll put my money on Charlotte. Josh must agree, because he raises both hands in surrender.

"I've already got a new teacher for you," Sister Stephanie tells us. The news inspires a sudden buzz and commotion that fills the room. "It is not Josh," she adds, "though I bet he could do a pretty good job."

Josh throws a big smile toward Charlotte, who just rolls her eyes.

When the room quiets down, Sister continues. "Before we talk about your new teacher, I want to make a couple of things very clear. First, what happened with Mr. DeGroot is not the fault of anybody in this room. He brought that on himself. Second, as far as the future of the band, I marched low brass when I was a student here. There will always be a marching band at St. Francis of Assisi High School as long as I am your principal."

Daniel hops onto his stronger leg and howls. *"Aroooo!"*

"Mr. Field," Sister says sharply, "despite my great love for the band, you probably don't want to bring yourself to my attention for a few days."

Daniel chokes back his cheer and drops into his seat almost before our principal completes the sentence.

Sister turns her attention to me. "That goes for you too, Miss Magari."

"Yes, Sister," I say.

Meanwhile, huge smiles cover every face in the room.

"So here's what we're going to do," Sister Stephanie continues. "I want everybody to take out their instruments." The clatter of horn cases, music stands, and shifting chairs nearly overwhelms the principal's voice, but she keeps going. "I want Hannah to come up here and do her drum major thing. I want the rest of you to play that jump-up-and-down song."

"'Jump on It!'" hollers Daniel.

Sister shoots him a stern look. "What did I tell you?"

"Sorry!" Daniel puts the piccolo to his mouth, lifts his eyes to the ceiling, and tries to look angelic.

Hannah steps to the front of the room. She's just about to count off when Sister Stephanie interrupts. "One more thing," she adds. "Your new band teacher is standing outside in the hallway. Be sure to make a good impression. And Mr. Field?"

Daniel is startled. "Yes, Sister?"

"Don't hold back."

"Yes, Sister!"

"READY?" shouts Hannah. "ONE! TWO! THREE!"

The brass explodes. Our percussion section goes crazy. I'm banging on a spare glockenspiel, but it still sounds great. At the drum break, Daniel dances and hops and spins like a wild animal possessed by the patron saint of caffeine. We approach the finale, and even Sister Stephanie is waving her hands in the air. We race into the song's final stanza like a battering ram smashing through a brick wall. I don't know if we have ever sounded this good. On the last note, the entire band bursts into spontaneous applause. That's when a small man wearing a pair of wrinkled cotton pants, worn loafers, and an untucked denim shirt slips into the room. He's clapping too. "Mr. Leary," Sister Stephanie says to him, "meet the band."

The man smiles at the class. "You can call me Billy."

"They can call you Mr. Leary," says Sister Stephanie.

He rolls his eyes. "Yes, Sister."

The principal socks Mr. Leary in the arm. "Don't 'Yes, Sister' me."

"But you're my sister."

The class sits up a little straighter.

"Mr. Leary is my brother," Sister Stephanie tells us. "That's why you will treat him with an abundance of respect."

Daniel raises his hand. "Which one of you is older?"

"Mr. Field," Sister Stephanie says to Daniel, "you must really want to join me after school for detention this week."

"She's older," says Billy Leary.

"I am not," says Sister.

Sinbad glances back and forth between our principal and her brother. "Wait a minute," he says out loud. "You're Billy Leary?"

"I am Billy Leary," the new teacher confirms.

"THE Billy Leary?"

"How many are there?" asks Charlotte. She turns to our new teacher. "Are you somebody?"

"You guys," Sinbad says to the class, "this is Billy Leary."

There is no reaction.

Mr. Leary turns to his sister. "Is this the abundance of respect you were talking about?"

"He was a big rock and roll star," Sinbad explains.

"I don't know if I'd go that far," says Sister Stephanie.

"Hey," Mr. Leary tells his sister, "don't interrupt the boy." Suddenly, our class finds this man who needs a haircut and looks as if he might sleep in his clothes a lot more interesting.

"My dad has one of your albums," Sinbad tells him.

Billy Leary gives him a smile. "You are officially my favorite student."

"We found it at a yard sale," Sinbad continues. "They were asking for a dollar, but he got it for fifty cents."

"The position of favorite student is available once more," Billy Leary announces to the class.

"Enough chitchat," says Sister Stephanie. "Mr. Leary— with the emphasis on *MISTER*—is a professional musician. He has worked with some very talented and well-known people. In fact, he's helped a lot of them to become better. I think he can do the same with you."

Hannah raises her hand again. "What instrument do you play?"

Mr. Leary gives a little shrug. "Pretty much all of them."

"At the same time?" asks Daniel.

Sister shoots a look at Daniel, who slides down in his seat.

"Mr. Leary is here because he is very kind," Sister informs us.

"I bet he's here because he's afraid of his sister," says Josh.

"Smart man," Charlotte and Sister Stephanie say at the exact same time.

"I came because I love to make music," Mr. Leary tells us. "Would anybody like to join me?"

Everybody's hands go up. Our new teacher turns to Sister Stephanie. "I can take it from here."

"You're sure?" she asks.

"This is the music room," Mr. Leary tells her. "These are my people."

CHAPTER 7: THE HISTORY OF THE GO-GO'S AND OTHER THINGS THAT MATTER

By lunchtime, rumors have convinced at least half our school that the new band teacher is Bruce Springsteen. The other half now believe that Sister Stephanie used to sing in an all-girl group called the Go-Go Girls. "Was she a Go-Go Girl before or after she joined the nuns?" asks Josh, who is eating a whole pizza for lunch.

Charlotte looks up from a history book propped between a water bottle and a banana. "You're kidding, right?"

"She was probably a Go-Go Girl before she was a nun," Josh says thoughtfully. "On the other hand, who says nuns can't be rock stars?"

"They weren't the Go-Go Girls," says Sinbad, who is

working on a set of math problems at the end of the table. "They were just the Go-Go's."

"Sinbad's right," I say. I know this is true because I stayed up late going through all the things stuffed into Mom's cardboard box. I studied the *CYNDI LAUPER'S NOT DEAD!* website too. Apparently, the name of her band must be capitalized, italicized, and always include an exclamation point at the end. I don't know why. In any case, *CYNDI LAUPER'S NOT DEAD (exclamation point!)* is a dedicated eighties tribute band. They play county fairs, music festivals, private functions, corporate outings, concert venues, and college campuses up and down the East Coast. Their set list definitely includes songs by the Go-Go's.

Daniel drops into a seat, shoves a handful of French fries into his mouth, then tries to speak. "Elles mom waf um rokumm bam."

"Translation?" says Charlotte.

"Ellie's mom was in a rock band," offers Anya Flowers, who has accepted an invitation from Daniel and me to join our lunch table.

"You understood him?" asks Charlotte.

Anya nods. "I speak four languages."

Josh turns to me. "Was your mom in the Go-Go's?"

I shake my head. "The Go-Go's came and went before my mom got to high school, but she sang their songs with her band."

Sinbad looks up. "Was she in an oldies group?"

"Sort of," I say.

"Nowzhy dead," adds Daniel, who's stuffed more French fries into his face.

Anya reaches across the table and gives him a whack.

Charlotte sits up. "What did he say?"

"Now she's dead," says Anya.

Charlotte turns to me. "Your mother is dead?"

"She is," I admit.

Charlotte reaches over and smacks Daniel again.

"What was that for?" he asks.

"Speaking about somebody's dead mom with your mouth full is rude." Charlotte turns back to her history text, reads a few lines, then closes the book. "You know what?" she says. "The history of the Go-Go's is much more interesting than the history of a bunch of dead white guys."

"The Go-Go's made history," says Sinbad. "They were the first all-girl band to become big stars while playing their own instruments and writing their own songs."

"Really?" says Charlotte.

"Absolutely."

"Are you sure?" I ask. "I mean they're old, but they're not that old."

"It was 1982," says Sinbad, who is apparently some kind of rock and roll encyclopedia, "and nobody did it before the Go-Go's."

"Why not?" asks Josh.

"Because boys," says Charlotte.

Sinbad nods. "That has a lot to do with it."

Daniel leans forward and interrupts the Go-Go's history lesson. "Do you guys want to help track down Ellie's mom?"

Josh looks confused. "I thought she was dead?"

"She is," I tell him. "But I never met her. She could be standing in the cafeteria right now, and I wouldn't recognize her."

"She'd be the dead one," offers Daniel.

Charlotte and Anya both whack him again.

"You don't know anything about her at all?" Josh asks me.

I shake my head. "I used to ask my dad, but he never said much."

Sinbad looks up from his math book. "So you just stopped asking?"

I think back to the few conversations I tried having with my father over the years. He was never mean or angry when I asked about my mom. Mostly, he just changed the subject. "Talking about it was kind of pointless," I say.

Charlotte surprises me by reaching across the table and taking my hand. "Listen, sweetie," she says. "Having a dead mom is a big deal. You've got to talk about it."

"How do you know?" Josh asks his sister. "Our mother isn't dead."

Charlotte shoots her brother an angry look. "A girl can dream."

Josh takes another piece of pizza. "You want our mother dead just because she yelled at you about your room this morning?"

Charlotte sighs. "No, I just want her to yell at you sometimes."

Josh bites into his pizza slice. "My room isn't a pigsty."

"It's not a pigsty if she knows where everything is," says Anya.

"Thank you," says Charlotte.

"Ellie," Sinbad says to me, "if I were you, I'd talk to him." He points toward the end of the cafeteria, where our new music teacher has just entered the room.

"Why would Mr. Leary know about my mother?" I ask.

"They're both musicians," Sinbad points out. "They're both from around here. They're both connected to St. Francis of Assisi High School. The odds of them knowing each other are better than zero."

Daniel turns to Sinbad. "I like the way you think."

"That does make sense," says Anya.

Sinbad waves across the room. "Mr. Leary," he calls. "Can we ask you a question?"

"What can I do for you?" our new teacher asks when he gets to our table.

"Was Sister Stephanie in the Go-Go's?" asks Josh.

Mr. Leary takes one of Daniel's French fries. "Yes," he says. "She was."

Charlotte picks up her banana and points it at the man. "Are you lying?"

"Yes," says Mr. Leary. "I am."

My stomach growls, reminding me of the lunch I left behind this morning. I steal a French fry for myself. "That's not really what we wanted to ask you."

Mr. Leary smiles. "I can handle more than one request."

"Did you know Ellie's mother?" asks Anya.

Mr. Leary scans the table. "Remind me which one of you is Ellie."

I raise my hand. "That's me. I'm Ellie Magari."

"Of course," he says. "The glockenspiel killer."

I am committed to ignoring all glockenspiel jokes, so I press on. "My mom went to school here," I tell him. "Her name was Wilma Korkenderfer. She graduated a couple years after Sister Stephanie. Until recently, she was the lead singer for an eighties tribute band called *CYNDI LAUPER'S NOT DEAD!*"

"Seriously?" says Charlotte.

Mr. Leary laughs. "I'll have to share that with Cyndi Lauper."

"You know Cyndi Lauper?" says Sinbad.

"She's one of the most beautiful, kind, and caring people in the world," Mr. Leary tells us. "Her voice is an instrument made out of God's own breath."

"Did you know my mom?" I ask.

Mr. Leary nods. "I'm four years older than Sister Stephanie, so I was already out of high school by the time your mother got here, but I needed backup singers for a demo track I was recording back then. I used a few singers from the St. Francis of Assisi High School choir to help me out. Korky Korkenderfer was one of them."

"Really?" I say. "You remember her?"

"I remember everybody I have ever fired."

Charlotte gets to her feet. "You fired my girl's dead mother? What's wrong with you, Mr. Leary?"

Mr. Leary takes a step back. "What are you talking about? Who's dead? I had to fire her. She was a terrible backup singer."

"Wilma Korkenderfer died two weeks ago," I explain.

Our new teacher puts a hand over his heart and drops into a plastic seat beside our table. "I am so sorry."

I never realized how many apologies are required to talk about dead people. "It's really okay," I tell him. "She and my dad split up when I was just a baby. I never met her."

"Ellie's trying to figure out where she comes from," says Charlotte.

"She's trying to figure out her story," adds Anya.

That's not how I would have explained what I'm doing. Actually, I have no idea how to explain what I'm doing. Maybe that's why I need help from Sichuan, Puerto Rico, Rockhill, and all points in between to figure it out.

"I didn't know her very well," Mr. Leary tells us. "That was a long time ago."

"Did you really fire her because she was a terrible singer?" I ask. Based on the fact that Wilma Korkenderfer led her own band for over a decade, I can't imagine how this can be true.

Mr. Leary shakes his head. "That's not what I said. That girl had a massive, powerful voice. It shook the fillings in your teeth. But she was young, and she didn't know how to use her instrument. Plus, I didn't know enough back then to teach her. Frankly, I don't know if she was teachable. But having her sing backup was like bringing in seventy-six trombones to play the lullaby at preschool nap time. It just wasn't going to work."

I consider this scarecrow of a man in front me. "You really know a lot about music, don't you?"

"That's what I tell people." Mr. Leary grins and gestures at the high school cafeteria around us. "It's gotten me this far."

Charlotte raises an eyebrow. She glances around the room, which smells like grilled cheese with a hint of lip gloss. "You must really love it a lot."

"I do," he admits.

"But how do you make it your job?" Sinbad asks him. "How did you become a professional musician?"

Mr. Leary turns to Sinbad. "Is that something you'd like to do?"

Sinbad glances at all of us around the table, then nods. "I'm thinking about it."

"I don't think there's a big need for professional snare drummers," says Josh.

"You'd be surprised," says Mr. Leary.

"I only picked up the snare so I could join marching band," Sinbad tells us. "My real instrument is guitar."

"But there's no marching guitars," I say.

Sinbad nods. "Exactly."

"That's how I got the glockenspiel," I tell him. "I play the piano."

Mr. Leary pushes his chair away from the table and stands. "Personally, I've always thought there should be marching pianos."

"I'd like to see that," says Josh.

"But seriously," Sinbad says to Mr. Leary. "How did you get here?"

"I went to college," Mr. Leary tells him. "I studied music. I spent several years in vans and buses with other people's concert tours. I moved to Nashville and then Austin. I helped friends make records. I made a few of my own. I finally moved to California because a lot of music happens there. I ended up doing tons of studio work, then started writing television scores and cleaning up movie soundtracks. A few years ago, I realized I could do that stuff from anywhere, so I moved back to Rockhill. Then, yesterday, I got a call from my sister congratulating me on my promotion to high school music teacher." He holds both hands out and gives a little shrug. "This is what it looks like when you're living the dream."

"You live in Rockhill?" says Charlotte.

Mr. Leary nods. "My backyard is Rockhill Memorial Cemetery."

"Mine too," says Daniel. "Anya and Ellie are just as close."

"My house is the one with the big red barn in the back," says Mr. Leary. "I built a recording studio there."

"Can we come and see it?" asks Sinbad.

Mr. Leary considers the question. "I'll have to ask my sister if that's allowed."

Charlotte peels her banana and takes a bite. "Mr. Leary," she says, "your life does not sound very rock and roll to me."

"I've got a tattoo," Mr. Leary informs her. "Does that count for something?"

"My mother is covered in tattoos," Sinbad tells us. "She's a dental hygienist."

Mr. Leary rolls up a sleeve and shows us a small black kite inked on the inside of his arm. "I got mine after a night out in Dublin with my friend David Evans." He points at the kite's tail, which is wrapped around the letter *U* and the number 2. "David is better known as the Edge."

Sinbad studies the tattoo. Our rock and roll encyclopedia leans back, smiles, and asks, "The edge of what?"

Mr. Leary stares at Sinbad for a moment. He opens his mouth as if to say something, then closes it again. Finally, he starts to walk away but stops and turns back. "What do they teach you in this school?"

"Mr. Leary," Charlotte replies. "That's up to you now."

CHAPTER 8: CONFUSION IS NOTHING NEW

The next morning, we find Mr. Leary standing atop a desk in the center of the music room. "What are you doing up there?" Daniel asks him.

Our teacher reaches up and pokes at the ceiling-mounted projector. "How do you turn this thing on?"

I walk to the front of the room, find the remote on a shelf, and hold it up for Mr. Leary to see. "You're supposed to use this." I push a green button, and Mr. Leary gets blasted in the face with a million-watt bulb.

"Shut it off! Shut it off!" he cries.

"Sorry!" I say.

By the time the rest of our class joins us, Mr. Leary is back on the ground and no longer blinded by the light. He's got the projector working properly, and a photograph of four guys with bad haircuts, cheesy mustaches, and cartoon-colored sailor suits shines on the whiteboard at the front of the room. "Find your seats," Mr. Leary announces. "We're starting the day with a pop quiz." He chuckles. "Because it's about pop. And it's a quiz."

Nobody else laughs.

"Never mind." He points at the image. "Raise your hand if you can identify these boys."

Less than half the class raises their hands.

"Seriously?" says Mr. Leary.

"It's the Beatles!" shouts Sinbad.

"Ten points for the kid who couldn't identify the Edge."

"The edge of what?" somebody whispers.

A black-and-white photo replaces the mustache quartet. Now we're looking at four scraggly-looking white guys standing in front of a dead tree in the middle of a desert. Sinbad's hand shoots up.

"Go on," Mr. Leary tells him.

"From left to right," says Sinbad. "That's Larry Mullen, Bono Hewson, Adam Clayton, and David Evans, who is also known as the Edge. Together, they are the band called U2. The Edge is the lead guitarist. My parents took me to see them in concert. My mom freaked out when I told her about your tattoo."

Mr. Leary's mouth drops open.

Sinbad gives Mr. Leary a big grin. "I was just messing with you yesterday."

Mr. Leary leans back against his desk. "New rules," he announces. "This quiz is just for Mr. Sinbad. If he gets them all right—"

Sinbad interrupts. "Then I get to teach everybody a song."

"What?" says Mr. Leary.

"If I get them all right, you let me teach a song to the class." Sinbad turns to face everybody. "But you guys really have to do it, okay?"

"I'll do it," says Josh.

Charlotte yells, "Go for it, Sinbad!"

"It's a deal," says Mr. Leary.

"I have to warn you," Sinbad tells our teacher. "My parents have a great record collection."

"Vinyl?" asks Mr. Leary.

Sinbad nods. "I told you. You're in it!"

Mr. Leary starts flashing new pictures on the board. Sinbad shouts out names to go with the photos. "Ray

Charles. Bo Diddley. Roy Orbison. Bob Dylan. The Beach Boys. Aretha Franklin. The Rolling Stones. Jimi Hendrix. Tina Turner."

"Not bad," says Mr. Leary. "But those were easy ones."

"Bring it on," says Sinbad.

The pictures start again. The very first one appears to stump our classmate.

"Give up?" Mr. Leary asks him.

Sinbad shakes his head. "The band is Cream. That's a young Eric Clapton on the right. The other two guys are Jack Bruce and Ginger Baker. I just don't know which one is Jack and which one is Ginger."

Mr. Leary rolls his eyes. "I'll give it to you."

The pictures continue. "David Bowie," says Sinbad. "Funkadelic, Bruuuuuuce, Michael Jackson." He looks at Mr. Leary. "Seriously? You didn't think we'd know Michael Jackson?"

"Five more to go," says Mr. Leary.

"Beastie Boys, Talking Heads, Prince." Sinbad laughs. "I bet Prince never thought he'd be on a Catholic school quiz."

"Two more."

"Nirvana."

The final slide appears. An intense girl with wild orange hair, ruby lipstick, a handful of flowers, and a cherry-red taffeta dress dances in fishnet stockings on a dirty sidewalk. I know this one.

"Cyndi Lauper!" Sinbad announces.

It feels like the entire class turns to look at me. It's probably just Daniel, Anya, Charlotte, and Josh. Still, the next thing I know, I'm crying. I'm crying so hard that tears actually make a puddle on my desk.

"Whoa!" says Charlotte.

"I'm sorry," I choke out.

"What happened?" somebody asks.

"Her mom died," Daniel whispers.

"Your mom was Cyndi Lauper?" Hannah Shupe asks me.

I shake my head. "Cyndi Lauper's not dead." I don't add the exclamation point.

After school, I sit alone in my room with the contents of Mom's shoe box spread across the bed. I'd considered inviting Anya or Charlotte to come over and go through it with me, but then I worried about what they might think of my bedroom. Beneath a window that looks down on the front yard, my desk is perfectly clean. Actually, I keep the windows spotless too. Framed posters from symphony orchestras and music conservatories cover my walls. I organize titles on my bookshelves by topic and author. From what I know of Anya and Charlotte, they'd probably find this kind of orderliness a little disturbing.

When it comes to staying organized, I guess I take after Dad, who believes in *mise en place*, a French term that describes how a chef is supposed to maintain a kitchen. Basically, *mise en place* means putting everything in its place. Ingredients, tools, menus, even your state of mind, should be arranged as cleanly, clearly, and efficiently as possible. For a lot of chefs, including Dad, *mise en place* goes way beyond the kitchen. It's a way of life.

Looking at the random collection in front of me, I suspect that Wilma Korkenderfer was more *mess en place* than *mise en place*. There doesn't seem to be any rhyme or reason to what she sent me. In fact, it would be easy to believe that this is nothing but a bunch of haphazard junk. But a set of handwritten lines scrawled inside the shoe box lid makes me believe that it's something more.

> *Lying in my bed I hear the clock tick,*
>
> *And think of you*
>
> *Caught up in circles*

Confusion is nothing new

Flashback—warm nights—

Almost left behind

Suitcases of memories,

Time after—

It's the first verse from a Cyndi Lauper song called "Time after Time." But what is it supposed to mean? Did my mother lie in bed thinking of me? Is the shoe box supposed to be a suitcase of memories? Either way, I'm glad to hear that confusion is nothing new. At least there's something I can say I share with my mother, because I am seriously confused.

I pick up a Flock of Seagulls CD. The lead singer's hair reminds me of the hat on Sister Stephanie's flying nun poster. I don't have a cassette or CD player, so I use my phone to listen to songs from the bands that Korky stuffed in the box. A Flock of Seagulls sounds like a couple of guys singing harmony on top of a sci-fi soundtrack. The Cure and Dead or Alive both scare me. I'm falling in love with Adam Ant, and a sickly sweet ballad by Spandau Ballet couldn't be more stuck in my head if the sheet music had been attached to a spear and shoved through my brain. Meanwhile, somebody named Boy George sounds like he wants to laugh and cry at the exact same time, and Cyndi Lauper might be even more amazing than Mr. Leary described.

None of this stuff is Mozart or Bach or Beethoven. Some of it is just plain bad. But there's also a lot that's fun, and challenging, and even wonderful. And for the most part, it's almost completely new to me.

Tapping my foot to a kooky, perfect pop song by a group called the Bangles, it strikes me that it's not just my mother that I've been missing. There's a whole wide world that I know nothing about.

CHAPTER 9: TRICK OR TREAT

On Friday, which is Halloween, Charlotte, Anya, Daniel, and I all dress like witches from the Wizard of Oz books. It was Anya's idea, so she's Glinda, the Good Witch of the South. Charlotte is Mombi, Wicked Witch of the West. I am decked out as Locasta, Good Witch of the North. That leaves Daniel dressed as Gingema, Wicked Witch of the East. Gingema is the witch who gets crushed when Dorothy falls out of the sky, so Daniel's costume is a tall cardboard box decorated to look like an old, brown house that's been dropped on his head.

"We're like a coven," says Charlotte when we gather around our cafeteria table at lunchtime.

"You need thirteen witches for a coven," Anya informs us.

"How do you know that?" I ask.

Anya smiles sweetly. "If I tell you, I'll have to turn you into a newt."

I turn my attention to Daniel. In addition to the box, he's wearing a pair of black-and-white striped stockings along with bright red, chunky-heeled Mary Janes decorated with a bow and glitter paint. "That's a good look for you," I tell him.

He makes an awkward twirl and nearly falls into a trash can.

Mr. Leary, who is wandering around the cafeteria and talking to costumed kids, approaches Daniel. "Is it just you and the girls today?"

Daniel clicks his bejeweled heels together. "Today, I am one of the girls."

Mr. Leary raises an eyebrow. "You think?"

Daniel does another little pirouette. When he spins, it looks as if his cardboard house is getting sucked up by a tornado and flushed down a toilet at the same time. Charlotte reaches out and pats him on the back door. "It takes more than good looks to be one of the girls, honey."

Daniel stops turning, kicks off his ruby slippers, and rubs the back of his foot against a metal chair leg. "To tell you the truth, this girl thing is killing me."

"You can rub a little lip balm on the backs of your heels to prevent blisters," Mr. Leary tells him.

Charlotte puts a black-gloved hand on one hip and tilts her head so that the top of her pointy black hat looks like a rocket launcher. "Is this what you learned from your rock star lifestyle?"

"First of all," says Mr. Leary, "I am not a rock star. Second of all, I spent six months touring with a hair-metal glam band, so I know how to be comfortable in heels. As far as the rock star lifestyle, Jon Bon Jovi bakes his own bread, Steven Tyler knits his own scarves, and Beyoncé gets ready to go onstage by practicing magic tricks."

"You're making that up," Daniel says from inside his box.

"Trust me," says Mr. Leary. "Beyoncé can pull silver dollars out of your ears all day long."

The bell announcing the end of the lunch period rings, and our conversation is nearly drowned out by laughing and shouting and scraping chairs as students begin cleaning up and heading toward the exits.

"Before you go," Mr. Leary tells us. "I checked with Sister Stephanie about school policy regarding students visiting teachers' homes. Basically, there should be another adult present. Your principal will be at my house tonight for Halloween, so feel free to come over."

"We're going trick-or-treating," Charlotte tells him.

"I give out good candy," Mr. Leary promises.

"Name brand and full-size?" she asks.

"Of course." Mr. Leary turns to me. "By the way, I found a copy of that CD your mom was supposed to sing on. Obviously, you won't hear her voice, but you can still have it if you want it."

"Okay," I say. "Thanks."

"Mr. Leary," Charlotte calls after our teacher, who is walking away now. "I don't care about Beyoncé's tricks, but you better not be lying about the good candy!"

Mr. Leary lifts a hand and gives a wave without turning around. "Happy Halloween!"

Several hours later, Anya, Charlotte, and I gather at the end of Daniel's driveway. Sinbad and Josh join us too. Even Hannah Shupe, our drum major, has come out. She's dressed as the Cowardly Lion. Sinbad and Josh are wearing Munchkin costumes, which almost works for Sinbad, but I don't recall any heavyweight wrestlers in Munchkin Country.

"Are you sure you want to trick-or-treat with underclassmen?" Daniel asks Hannah, who is a senior.

"I love trick-or-treating," she tells him. "And I couldn't find anybody else older than nine to go with me."

"It was a yes-or-no question," says Josh, who is holding a gigantic, round lollipop.

"What are you supposed to be?" Hannah asks him.

"I'm a Munchkin," Josh tells her.

She twirls her tail and studies Josh's huge outfit. "Are you sure you know what that word means?"

"People," hollers Charlotte, who is marching around in knee-high, black stilettos, "let's get started!"

"Who died and left her in charge?" asks Sinbad.

Anya points at Daniel's Wicked Witch of the East outfit. "Technically, he did."

A moment later, we join a crowd of small, one-eyed pirates, bloody zombies, and miniature superheroes moving through the neighborhood. I'm swinging a bright orange trick-or-treat bag in one hand. In the other, I've got a spatula that I'm using as my magic wand. A yellow half-moon shines through long oak and maple branches above us. "Does anybody know where we're going?" Hannah asks.

"There's a walking path at the end of the block," Daniel tells her. After a long day at school, his cardboard house looks like a stack of recycling that's been run over by a garbage truck. "It cuts through the cemetery and leads past the house with the red barn. That's got to be Mr. Leary's."

"Fly, monkeys! Fly!" cries Charlotte.

Daniel staggers down the sidewalk in his heels but comes to a stop at the narrow gate that leads into the cemetery.

"What's wrong?" I ask him.

"I'm not just as big as a house," he says. "I am a house."

"So?"

"So I don't fit through the gate."

"So get out of the house," I suggest.

"Good idea." Daniel pushes the cardboard over his head. It gets stuck briefly, but a strong gust of wind suddenly lifts the thing off his shoulders. The box flies for a moment, hits the ground, then collapses with a muffled *poof!*

"Your witching days are over," Anya tells him.

"I was already dead." Daniel kicks off his ruby slippers. "Now I'm free." He reaches into a small backpack that's slung over his shoulders and pulls out an old gray Trinity

College sweatshirt and a pair of sneakers with laces that match his pumpkin-orange gym shorts. Once his shoes are on, Daniel heads through the cemetery gate and into the graveyard. "Ellie," he calls back to me. "Don't be afraid. There's nothing in here but dead people."

"Thanks." If Daniel makes one more joke about dead people I'm going to have to kill him. And wouldn't that be ironic.

As he marches away, I glance back up our street and toward my house, where Dad is handing out homemade caramels to trick-or-treaters. He asked me if I'd stay home and help tonight, but I acted like a witch. And not a good one. As a matter of fact, we were yelling at each other before I headed out.

"Ellie," Charlotte calls from inside the cemetery. "Come on!"

I jog down the walking path and catch up with Anya and Sinbad, who are lagging behind the others. The three of us walk together past long lines of headstones. As we continue down the path, Anya points toward one inscription and starts to laugh. *"Optima medicina non est semper risus,"* she reads out loud.

"What's that mean?" says Sinbad.

"It's Latin for 'Laughter is not always the best medicine.'"

"You speak Latin?" asks Sinbad.

Anya shrugs. "It's a lot like Spanish."

Our friends are far ahead now, but I can see their shadows in the distance. When we finally catch up, Sinbad says, "Check it out!"

Anya and I join him in front of a large, stone statue of a fat, laughing Buddha. The figure, which is seated on a flat rock, holds both hands up in the air as if he is cheering us on. Anya leans forward and rubs the statue's round belly. "In China," she explains, "it's good luck to rub the happy Buddha's tummy."

In addition to rubbing the Buddha's stomach, Sinbad and I both give him gentle high fives. "Are there any happy Catholic saints?" I ask.

Sinbad looks around, then points at a small ceramic figure placed atop a nearby grave marker. "What about her?"

"That's Our Lady of Guadalupe," says Anya.

"Are you going to rub her tummy?" Sinbad asks me.

"I don't think so," I tell him.

"Why not?"

"That's Jesus's mother," I remind him. "The Virgin Mary. You don't rub the Virgin Mary's tummy."

Sinbad studies Our Lady of Guadalupe. "She looks very nice. I don't think she'd mind."

"Hey!" Hannah calls from up ahead. "Are you coming?"

"Well?" he says.

I take a step closer to the statue. What can it hurt? I tuck my magic spatula into my bag, then reach out to rub Mary's tummy with my palm. In the dark, however, I don't notice a low gravestone in the grass at my feet. I stumble over the granite marker, trip, and pitch forward. A moment later, I accidentally hit the Virgin Mary with all my weight. In other words, I've just approached Holy Mary, Mother of God, and punched her in the stomach.

Yay me.

The statue snaps off its base with a loud *CRACK!* Now I'm gripping Our Lady of Guadalupe in both hands. I hold the figure away from my body like it's a baby that needs a diaper change.

"What did you do?" asks a shocked Anya, whose eyes are as big as two full moons.

"I don't know!"

"Put it back!" she tells me.

I try to return the statue to its place, but the base is broken. "It won't go!"

"Then put her down!"

"I can't leave her here!"

"You guys!" Hannah's voice comes again from the distance. "Help!"

"Help?" I say.

"Come on!" says Sinbad.

I hold up the statue. "What about—"

"Put her in your bag!" says Sinbad.

"Help!" Hannah yells again.

"We're coming!" Sinbad shouts.

"Sorry," I say to Mary. I drop her into my trick-or-treat bag, then sprint after Anya and Sinbad toward Hannah's voice. Our Lady of Guadalupe slaps against my thigh as we race across the cemetery. Fortunately, it doesn't take long to reach Hannah, so the Virgin Mary and I both arrive without too much damage.

"Are you okay?" I ask Hannah, who stands by herself on the graveyard path.

"I wore the Cowardly Lion costume for a reason," she says. "And it's not because I enjoy being left alone in a cemetery at night." She points into the dark. "I heard a noise from over there."

Anya glances at the shadowy headstones all around us. "Where did everybody go?"

Hannah points toward the shadow of a barn at the edge of the cemetery.

"Is that Mr. Leary's?" asks Sinbad.

Hannah nods. "Daniel, Josh, and Charlotte ran ahead to see if he's home. But then I heard screaming."

"What were they screaming about?" asks Sinbad. "Why didn't you follow them?"

"Did I mention the Cowardly Lion costume?" says Hannah.

I turn toward the barn. "Let's go see if they're okay."

"I'll stay here," says Hannah.

"In the dark with Halloween ghosts, and graves, and dead people?" asks Anya.

Hannah grabs my hand. "I'll come with you."

Together, we make our way up a gentle slope toward Mr. Leary's barn. As we approach, we hear a familiar voice. It's Sister Stephanie, and she's not happy. "Do you have no experience with doors?" she is hollering. "People a lot less adept than you have figured out how to use them. Or have I overestimated your abilities?"

"No, Sister," says Josh.

"Yes, Sister," says Daniel at the exact same time.

Sinbad, Hannah, Anya, and I round the corner of the building. Sister Stephanie, dressed in full flying nun regalia, stands in front of the open barn door with Charlotte. Light from inside streams onto a patch of brown grass, where Josh and Daniel are sprawled on their backs.

"Trick or treat?" says Sinbad.

CHAPTER 10: *FEROCE! FURIOSO! FORTISSIMO!*

Mr. Leary steps out of the barn and into the light. "Happy Halloween!" He notices Josh and Daniel in the grass. "What are you doing down there?"

Daniel gets to his feet. He looks ridiculous in his pumpkin-colored gym shorts and striped witch stockings. "I was trying to make sure this was your house."

"Here's an idea," says Sister. "You could have knocked."

"I'm still confused," says Mr. Leary.

Josh stands and points at a half-moon window directly above the open barn door. "I let Daniel climb on my shoulders to look inside."

"Sister saw Daniel's face in the window," Charlotte explains.

"And then I opened the door," says Sister.

I glance at the entryway. "That door swings out."

"It sure does," says Josh, who is standing beside Daniel now. The two of them look like dogs who got caught peeing on the rug.

"It hit them like a sledgehammer," says Charlotte. "Josh got knocked right off his feet. Daniel flew like he'd been launched out of a catapult." She turns to Sister Stephanie. "You don't know your own strength, Sister."

Sister rolls her eyes. "Seeing one of your students' faces hovering in a window ten feet off the ground on Halloween night can really get the adrenaline flowing."

"She went into total exorcist mode," Charlotte tells us.

"Miss Rios," says Sister Stephanie, "in my line of work, we're not big fans of exorcism jokes."

"Sorry," says our very own Wicked Witch of the West.

Mr. Leary laughs. "Please, come inside!"

As we head into the barn, Sister Stephanie stands in the doorway and drops candy into our bags. I'm last in line, and when it's my turn, she holds out three extra-large chocolate bars. "Ellie Magari," says Sister, "we had a rough week, but that doesn't mean I don't like you a lot."

"Thank you," I say.

"You're welcome."

I open my Halloween bag. Sister drops the candy. The chocolate bars hit Our Lady of Guadalupe on the head. *Clunk. Clunk. Clunk.* Sister reaches into the bag and pulls out the statue. For a long moment, neither one of us speaks. Finally, Sister breaks the silence. "Holy Mary, Mother of God, what are you doing here?"

I consider all the possible answers to this question. As it works out, there aren't many. "It's not what you think," I say.

Sister holds up the broken statue. "I think I just found Our Lady of Guadalupe in your trick-or-treat bag."

"Okay," I say. "It is what you think, but I can explain."

"Please do."

In a rush, I tell her about our walk through the graveyard, and the Buddha, and the fact that laughter is not always the best medicine. And then I explain how Hannah, who really is a cowardly lion, started screaming, and how I tripped, causing me to knock Mary off her pedestal. Somehow, I include the part about rubbing a lucky tummy, and I admit that I'm concerned about the apparent lack of happy Catholic saints. Before I know it, I'm going on about my stupid father and my dead mother and Cyndi Lauper, whose voice really is an instrument made out of God's own breath. I also explain that I wish my parents—both the live one and the dead one—had trusted me instead of keeping a lifetime's worth of secrets. And I'm wondering if maybe my mother might actually be buried somewhere in Rockhill Memorial Cemetery, and I confess that I'd always hoped to meet my mom one day, but now that's never going to happen, and—

"Ellie," says Sister.

"What?"

She presses Our Lady of Guadalupe into my arms. "Keep the statue."

"Should I put her back in the cemetery?"

Sister shakes her head. "You need her a lot more than anybody who's already buried."

"What am I going to do with a statue of the Virgin Mary?" I ask.

Sister puts her hand on my shoulder. "You'll figure something out."

I place Mary back into the bag and follow Sister Stephanie into the barn. Looking around, I realize that Mr. Leary wasn't kidding about the professional recording studio. Charlotte is seated behind a massive set of drums. Josh and Anya are making weird electronic sounds with some kind of keyboard. Daniel has discovered a piccolo, and Sinbad is showing Hannah how to make a chord on a cherry-red electric guitar shaped like a lightning bolt. Meanwhile, a half dozen old upright pianos stand in a line against the barn's back wall.

"Does Mr. Leary collect pianos?" I ask Sister Stephanie, who is now in the middle of the room.

"He rescues them," she tells me. "Whenever he hears about a piano that somebody's going to throw away, he runs over, grabs it, and brings it back here."

"Why would anybody throw away a perfectly good piano?"

"They are not perfectly good," says Sister. "Most of them aren't even good."

"Ellie," Mr. Leary calls to me. He's standing beside a tall bookshelf filled with old magazines and stacks of compact discs. He flips through the pile, finds what he's looking for, then turns and hands a CD to me. "Here's that recording. It's probably your mom's first professional credit."

The CD case is made out of heavy paper and decorated like a hand-drawn chessboard. Three names fill a white square labeled EXTRA VOICES. I read them out loud. "Seamus

Brady, Ranking Richard, and Wilma Korkenderfer." I look up at Mr. Leary. "Wilma and Seamus got married. They're the ones that started *CYNDI LAUPER'S NOT DEAD!*"

"I don't remember Seamus Brady," Mr. Leary confesses.

"You must not have fired him," says Charlotte, who has crossed the barn to join us. She glances at the CD in my hand. "What kind of name is Ranking?"

Mr. Leary shakes his head. "It's a Jamaican nickname. It means 'well respected,' but that kid was no more Jamaican than I am. He kept trying to convince me to give everything a reggae beat. Ranking Richard was very annoying, but he was a pretty good singer and a talented horn player too. To tell the truth, I should have listened to that boy. Ska music was the next big thing about a year later."

"Whatever happened to Mr. Ranking?" says Charlotte.

Sister Stephanie exchanges a quick glance with her brother. "One day I will tell you all about Ranking Richard," she promises. "But not today."

"Mr. Leary," I ask, "why did you leave Wilma's name on the credits if she's not actually on the CD?"

Mr. Leary shrugs. "Music is a tough business. I thought having a credit might help her one day."

"That was a good deed," Charlotte tells him.

"It wasn't much," says Mr. Leary. "It didn't cost me anything."

"See," I say to Sister Stephanie, who is struggling to pin the hat part of the flying nun costume back on her head. "Good deeds don't have to cost anything."

Sister lifts the big white cowl, which has tilted forward and covered her face. "Good deeds don't have to come with rewards either."

"I didn't expect any rewards," I protest.

"I know that. Now apply those same zero expectations to costs, and I promise you'll have a much happier life." She whips the flying nun hat off and flings it onto a nearby chair. "I really hate that thing."

Mr. Leary laughs. "My sister isn't the Buddha quite yet."

"Show me a Buddha in a wimple," says Sister, "and I'll show you somebody who's still a long way from nirvana."

I tuck the CD into my bag with the Virgin Mary, then wander over to the wall to take a closer look at the pianos. They're all dented and worn. Several are missing keys. One has a hole in its side that might have been created by a sledge-hammer or maybe a shotgun blast. Compared to these, my

Lester belongs in Carnegie Hall. I take a seat at one piano that's got a brick holding up a back corner. I play a couple of quick scales along with a few major chords. Imagine a dying cow singing beached whale song while kicking a set of broken wind chimes. That's what this piano sounds like.

"Is that awesome or what?" Mr. Leary asks me.

"I think it's more what than awesome," I say.

Mr. Leary pulls a chair up to the piano right next to mine. "Every good piano sounds roughly the same," he tells me. "But no two old pianos ever sound alike. Each one finds its own distinct voice. And when you play them together—"

He starts plunking out "The Celebrated Chop Waltz," better known as "Chopsticks," so I join in.

"It's like a choir of frogs and crickets," he continues. "You wouldn't think bugs and amphibians could sound good, but they do."

Sister Stephanie takes a third piano and starts to play along.

"You play?" I ask her.

She gives a little smile. "I can hold my own."

We start slowly, but before I know it, the simple waltz, originally written by a sixteen-year-old girl in nineteenth-century Britain, has become a full-on, rocking piano duel between Mr. Leary, Sister, and me. We trade fancy runs and syncopated rhythms and show-off variations. My friends clap and cheer. Daniel provides a Wolf Pack howl. *"Aroooo!"*

The action on my keyboard is mushy and dense, so I'm hitting every note with all my strength. Finally, one key actually pops off the piano and clatters to the ground. This makes Mr. Leary laugh so hard that he simply comes to a stop. "I give up!" he cries. "I give!"

I look at Sister Stephanie, who raises an eyebrow, then nods toward my hands. I look down and see a red streak across a couple of keys. I must have cut a finger on the jagged edge left behind by the broken note. I remember the sign on Sister's office wall. "Somebody may beat me," I say, "but they are going to have to bleed to do it."

Sister shakes her head and takes her hands away from the piano keys. "You win."

"Feroce! Furioso! Fortissimo!" says Mr. Leary, who is still laughing. *Feroce, furioso,* and *fortissimo* are piano terms that instruct a musician to play ferociously, furiously, and very, very loud. "You know, you play the same way your mother sang," he adds.

"No," I say a little breathlessly. "I didn't know."

He gives me a big smile. "Now you do."

CHAPTER 11: NOT HOW STORIES WORK

When I get home, I find Dad in the kitchen stabbing a hole in a wall with an old chef's knife. "What are you doing?" I ask.

"I'm looking for the wooden part behind the plaster."

"The stud?"

"Whatever. It needs to hold up a shelf."

"You're making a shelf?" Despite his ability to make magic with saucepots and frying pans, Dad is not handy when it comes to home repair.

He finds a pencil and makes a little mark on the wall. "It's not going to make itself."

"Wait till tomorrow," I say. "We can work on it together."

"Now you want to do something together?"

It's possible Dad is still angry that I left him alone for Halloween.

"You're the cook, not the carpenter." Thanks to several million how-to videos on YouTube, I'm usually the one in charge of fix-it projects and repair jobs. "Let me help."

Dad grabs a hammer off the kitchen table. "Carpenters make things. Cooks make things. I've got this, Ellie."

I take the hammer out of Dad's hands. "Birds make eggs, but you wouldn't ask a parakeet to cook an omelet."

"I bet I could teach a crow to grill a burger," he tells me.

"I'll grill you a burger if you let me do the shelf."

"I don't need a burger," Dad says. "I need pizza. Actually, I need a pizza truck. I found out yesterday that Trinity College is going to offer pizza on wheels in the spring."

I don't understand at first. "Did they steal your idea?"

Dad shakes his head. "I told my boss about Pizza Alato! about a year ago. He liked it a lot. We've been working to make it part of Trinity's food service program. We learned yesterday that everything's been approved. Starting next year, Pizza Alato! is going to be at Trinity football games, reunion weekends, homecoming, and special events all over campus."

"Wow!" I drop into a kitchen chair. "That's amazing!"

Dad takes a seat across from me. "Not only that, I can suggest that they sell the business to me in a few years. I was hoping to tell you all about it when we handed out trick-or-treat candy together."

"Oh."

He points at the wall where the shelf will go. "I want to make some storage space for the pizza stuff."

"Please let me help you with that," I say again.

Dad stares at the wall, then turns back to me. "Okay."

"Thank you."

Dad points at my Good Witch costume. "Glinda?"

"Locasta."

"Very nice."

"We went to Mr. Leary's house."

"Billy Leary?" asks Dad.

"He's Sister Stephanie's brother."

"I know that."

"He's our music teacher now."

"He used to be a big rock and roll star," says Dad.

"He says not so big." I reach into the trick-or-treat bag I left on the floor. I pull out the CD from Mr. Leary and hand it to my father. "He gave me this."

Dad takes it.

"Wilma Korkenderfer's name is on it," I tell him.

Dad examines the disc, then slides it back across the table. "Okay."

"Okay?"

Dad shrugs. "Okay."

"That's all you have to say about it?"

"What do you want me to say, Ellie?"

"I—" I stop. "I have no idea."

"Guess what," he says. "Neither do I."

I take the CD and drop it back into the bag. "It doesn't matter. She didn't sing on any of the songs."

"Too bad," Dad says.

"Do you want to know why?"

"Not really," he tells me.

"Would you listen to the CD if she was on it?"

Dad actually considers the question. "Maybe. Korky had a great voice." Dad points at the wood and the tools spread on the floor. "You promise you'll help me with this tomorrow?"

"Are you going to change the subject every time I try to talk about her?"

"I'm not working in the morning, so we can do it first thing."

"Fine," I say. "We'll put up your shelf, and then I'm going to spend the afternoon with my friends. They're helping me learn about my mother."

Dad reacts as if he's been punched in the face. "No."

"But—"

"But nothing," Dad says. "She didn't come back when she was alive. She didn't call back when she was dying. She doesn't get a triumphant return because she's dead."

"Wait," I say. "You knew she was dying?"

"Ellie," says Dad in an exasperated voice. "I called Seamus when the box arrived."

"You know about Seamus?"

Dad rolls his eyes. "We all grew up together. We all went to high school together. They have a website, for God's sake. It wasn't too hard to track them down."

"Did you talk to—"

Dad shakes his head. "Korky was sleeping when I called. I told Seamus not to wake her, but I left a message that I wanted to talk about that box. She never called back. She'd started treatments, and Seamus warned me that they made her very tired. He also told me she was absolutely certain she was going to beat it. Of course she was certain. Korky was always absolutely certain about everything. She probably meant to call back once she got a clean bill of health so she could let me know how she'd won again. Or else she planned to call during her final minutes so we could all play out some kind of dramatic scene filled with apologies and forgiveness. I bet she worked on her last words for weeks. But you know what?"

"What?" I say.

"You can't rehearse the future, and you can't rearrange the past." Dad stands. "Korky's the one who walked out. She could have come back anytime. She didn't. End of story."

I think back to Anya rearranging pictures and scenes on her wall. "I'm really sorry," I tell my father, "but that's not how stories work."

Dad stares at me for a long moment. Without speaking, he finally turns and leaves.

"Apparently, Korky isn't the only one who liked a dramatic scene!" I holler after him.

I get no reply.

I reach into the orange trick-or-treat bag, pull out Our Lady of Guadalupe, and set her in the middle of the kitchen table where I'm sure Dad will notice. Maybe she can talk some sense into him.

CHAPTER 12: A LESSON ABOUT WAFFLES

It's barely half past seven when the *kabang!* of a dropped hammer plus a loud *"Dammit!"* from downstairs ends my dreams of sleeping late on Saturday. When Dad agreed to build the shelf in the morning, I assumed we'd begin at a more reasonable time. On the other hand, this probably feels reasonable to the man who usually leaves the house before the sun comes up.

"I'll be right down!" I shout.

I find a pair of jeans, a sweatshirt, and a baseball cap. I don't see my shoes, so I slip into a pair of fuzzy bunny slippers. In the bathroom, I brush my teeth and wash my face as fast as I can, then head downstairs. When I get to the kitchen, Dad's not there but Our Lady of Guadalupe stands on a brand-new, surprisingly strong-looking shelf looking over the room.

"Dad?" I holler.

No answer.

"Anybody home?" I yell.

Still nothing.

I can't believe he would have left the house without telling me. I open the door that connects the kitchen to the garage. Dad's car is gone. I turn to the statue of Guadalupe. "So that's how it's going to be?" I ask out loud.

Mary doesn't answer, so I go back to my room and trade my slippers for a pair of sneakers. While I tie my laces, I glance around my bedroom with everything in its place and a place for everything. Only a week ago, my whole life felt this orderly. Then Wilma Korkenderfer arrived and everything went to pieces. How do people live like this? I think of Anya and her jumbled pile of books and movies and pandemonium. Maybe I need to visit her and ask for a list of chaos survival techniques.

I stand and glance out my window at Daniel's house. There's no sign of movement. Mrs. Field's car is gone. I'm sure she's already at work. Daniel could still be asleep, but he's usually an early riser, so I decide to head across the street. Before I turn away from the window, however, a small green sedan turns into our neighborhood. It passes below my window and heads all the way into the dead end. In the cul-de-sac, the car makes a U-turn and starts coming back down the block. For some reason, it comes to a stop at the end of our driveway. The glare from the morning sun prevents me from seeing inside, but it seems as if the driver might be examining my mailbox.

Just then, Daniel, wearing lobster-print pajama bottoms and an oversize sweatshirt that says ALWAYS ORGANIC FRUIT, bursts out of his front door. He races toward the street, yelling and waving what appears to be a large green zucchini. Before Daniel reaches the curb, the car pulls away.

I have no idea what that was about, but at least I know Daniel's awake.

I head across the street and find Daniel waiting just inside his front door. "Get in here!" he yells.

"What's wrong?" I ask.

"Hurry up!" He grabs my shoulder and nearly pulls me off my feet before he slams the door shut.

Daniel's house is built according to the exact same plan as mine, but it really couldn't be more different. A huge TV hangs on the wall of a very messy living room that's filled with a couple of mismatched couches and several overstuffed chairs. In the kitchen down the hall, the only appliances Mrs. Field uses regularly are the coffeepot, the refrigerator, and the microwave. Upstairs, Daniel's bedroom holds nothing but a mattress on the floor and bookshelves made from wood planks and cement blocks. Still, this place is as much a home to me as my own house. I drop into one of the chairs. "What's the emergency?"

"Mr. DeGroot was here!" he says.

That gets my attention. "What?"

"He was cruising down our street."

"Was that him in the green car?"

Daniel nods. "He stopped in front of your house. I chased him away."

I glance at a coffee table, where there's a long green squash that's as thick as my arm. "With a zucchini?"

Daniel plops onto an empty couch. "I didn't have time to find a glockenspiel."

"What was he looking for?" I wonder.

"He was looking for you!" Daniel exclaims. "He wants revenge!"

"Don't be ridiculous."

"It's not ridiculous when the angry man who got fired because of you parks outside your house," says Daniel.

"He didn't actually do anything," I point out.

Daniel picks up the zucchini and waves it threateningly. "Thanks to this."

"Unless Mr. DeGroot has a serious gourd allergy, I don't know why he'd run away from a zucchini."

"We should tell somebody," says Daniel.

"What would we tell them? That our old music teacher drove down our street?"

"What about the day we were looking for the piccolo?" says Daniel. "He showed up then too."

"We were at school. He worked there."

"He'd just been fired."

"He probably had to clean out his desk."

"Is your father home?" Daniel asks me.

"He's not home," I say, "and you're overreacting."

Daniel leans back on the couch and tosses the zucchini straight into the air. The big squash tumbles end over end and then falls straight back into his hands. "Maybe we should call the police."

"You watch too much *Law and Order*."

Daniel throws the zuke again. This time he gives it a little too much zip. It hits the ceiling, ricochets off a wall, and nearly knocks me in the head.

"You're way more dangerous than Mr. DeGroot," I say.

Daniel sits up. "At least call Sister Stephanie."

"You're not that dangerous," I tell him.

"Just let her know that we think Mr. DeGroot might be stalking us."

"But I don't think that," I point out.

"You can say you think it's nothing but that I disagree. Also, if we disappear, she should look for our bodies in the cemetery."

"Why the cemetery?" I ask.

Daniel retrieves the zucchini, which now has a big dent in it. He places it back on the coffee table. "Can you think of a better place to hide a dead body?"

"Good point," I admit. "Plus, we're going to cut across the cemetery on our way to Anya's, so that's where he'll probably catch us and kill us."

"Not funny," says Daniel. "When are we going to Anya's?"

"How about now?"

"How about you call Sister Stephanie first?"

"How about not?"

"But—"

"Daniel," I say, "I'm the girl that threw a glockenspiel for you. You're the boy that just chased a car with a zucchini for me. We've got each other's backs."

"Well," says Daniel. "When you put it like that."

A few minutes later, we're standing on Anya's front step. Daniel, still in his fruit farm sweatshirt and lobster-print pajamas, rings the bell. After a short wait, Anya's father opens the door. He's wearing a UMASS sweatshirt and the exact same pajama bottoms as Daniel.

"Nice jammies," Daniel tells him.

"Thank you." Dr. Flowers takes a sip from the coffee cup in his hand. "What can I do for you?"

"We're here to see Anya," says Daniel.

"Is she home?" I ask.

"She's still in bed," he tells us.

I hadn't considered that. "Oh."

"We're early risers," Daniel tells him.

"As am I." Dr. Flowers takes another sip of coffee. "Would you like to come in? Mrs. Flowers went grocery shopping, but I can make you a waffle."

"I like waffles," says Daniel.

Dr. Flowers gestures for us to follow, and we enter the foyer, head past the room with the beautiful piano, and step into the Flowers' big kitchen, where we find Anya sitting at the kitchen table. "Are you the ones that rang the doorbell?" she asks sleepily.

"Sorry," I say.

Dr. Flowers crosses the room to a big, silver refrigerator in the corner. He opens the freezer and pulls out a bright yellow box of frozen waffles. "Oh no," says Daniel. "That won't do."

"What's wrong?" asks Dr. Flowers.

"Those aren't waffles," Daniel tells him. "That's barely even food. What kind of doctor are you?"

"I have degrees in history from Amherst and Chicago, and a PhD from Yale. I think I know the difference between food and not food."

Daniel points at the box. "You might know who shot Lincoln, but you don't know waffles."

"Do you teach at Trinity College?" I ask.

"I'm the chair of the history department," says Dr. Flowers. "But apparently I'm not qualified to toast a waffle."

Daniel shakes his head. "You don't toast a waffle. You mix a simple batter in a bowl, then pour it over a hot griddle and cook until golden brown."

"My dad works at Trinity," I say. "He runs the morning and lunch shifts in the cafeteria. He and Daniel like to cook together."

Dr. Flowers studies me for a moment. "Is your dad Bruce Magari?"

"That's him."

"Bruce speaks to my medieval history class every year about bread. That man knows more about bread than I know about the Battle of Pinkie Cleugh. And I know a lot."

"Pinkie what?" asks Daniel.

"The Battle of Pinkie Cleugh," says Dr. Flowers. "It was part of the war known as the Rough Wooing between Henry VIII's British monarchy and the Scottish—"

"Dad," says Anya, "we don't want to hear about Pinkie Cleugh."

"It was a remarkable battle," Dr. Flowers tells Daniel, who actually looks sort of interested.

"How about bread pudding?" I ask. "But instead of bread, we'll use waffles."

"Frozen waffles?" says Daniel.

"Why not?" I take the yellow box from Dr. Flowers and guide him to a seat at the kitchen table. "You sit. We'll cook."

Rather than toast the waffles, I soften them in the microwave. Daniel tears them into pieces and tosses the bits into a baking dish. I tell Anya to bring milk, eggs, brown sugar, butter, cinnamon, raisons, and a dash of nutmeg, which we combine in a glass bowl. Daniel pours the mixture over the broken waffles, then stirs everything up in the baking dish and slides it into the oven.

"Do you have any maple syrup?" I ask.

Anya heads to a cabinet near the coffeepot. "I'll get it."

"Can I ask a question?" says Dr. Flowers.

"Food-related or otherwise?" asks Daniel.

"My question is for Ellie." Dr. Flowers turns to me. "I understand that you're searching for your mom."

I glance at Anya.

"I told my parents," she says. "I hope you don't mind. We talk about finding my biological parents one day."

"You talk about it?" I say. "Out loud?"

"Anya knows she's adopted," says Dr. Flowers. "Pretending otherwise would be absurd. And the fact that she has her own history makes it even more special that we are together now."

"I never thought of it like that," I admit.

"Did I mention that my dad is a history professor?" says Anya.

"Have you made any progress?" Dr. Flowers asks me.

"A little," I say.

Dr. Flowers nods. "Anya explained that your mother passed away before you ever had a chance to meet."

I nod.

"Was she from around here?"

"My parents grew up in Rockhill."

"Then your grandparents must have lived here too," says Dr. Flowers. "Did you know them?"

I shake my head. "They all died before I was born."

"Did your mom and dad have brothers or sisters?" he asks. "Any aunts? Uncles? Cousins?"

In our small town, even my father wouldn't be able to hide an entire clan from me. "I don't think so."

Just then, the doorbell rings. Anya steps out of the kitchen. When she returns, she's with her mom, who, like Anya, is carrying several bags of groceries. "I needed help with the door," says Mrs. Flowers. "And what is that amazing smell?"

"Frozen waffle pudding," Daniel tells her.

She raises an eyebrow.

"You'll like it," he promises.

"It will be ready in five minutes," I say.

"I'll be right back," says Dr. Flowers. He steps out of the kitchen while Anya and Mrs. Flowers begin unpacking groceries. He returns a moment later with a copy of the *Rockhill Free Press* and a fat yellow book, which he plops into my arms. The book weighs a ton.

"What's this?" I ask.

"A newspaper and a phone book," he says. "Hardly anybody uses them anymore. It's a shame. Fortunately, the library has copies going back a hundred years. The librarians can help you find news, obituaries, wedding announcements, city maps, and even school yearbooks. They'll lead to your mom. You just have to ask."

"That's a good idea," says Daniel.

"You won't be looking for a person at first," Dr. Flowers tells me. "You just collect clues and bits of information. When you have enough pieces, you can arrange them into a story that makes sense."

I turn to Anya. "Is this where you learned how to do that storyboard thing?"

"No," she says, "but it's not that different, is it?"

"It sounds like your family has been in town for at least a couple generations," Dr. Flowers continues. "They won't be able to hide for long."

The oven timer goes off, so I trade the newspaper and phone book for a pair of hot mitts. I move the baking dish from the oven to the countertop. While it cools, I add a generous helping of maple syrup and think about everything Dr. Flowers just said. A moment later, Daniel and I scoop servings into bowls.

"This smells delicious," says Mrs. Flowers.

"It used to be waffles," Dr. Flowers tells his wife.

Daniel leans toward Anya's mom and speaks in a loud whisper. "Mrs. Flowers," he says, "it was never waffles."

CHAPTER 13: HISTORY IS REAL LIFE

After the morning waffle lesson with Dr. Flowers, Daniel and I phone our friends. They agree to gather at the Rockhill Public Library to help explore my past. An hour later, we're all squeezed around a heavy, wooden table on the library's top floor. "Ellie," says Charlotte, who dragged Josh and Sinbad along, "what do you need us to do?"

Above us, an autumn sun shines through a tall, arched window that's been letting light into the library for over a hundred years. A few of the people sitting nearby look like they've been here that long too.

"It's sort of like working on a research paper," I explain.

"Wow," says Josh. "You really know how to have fun on a Saturday."

"It's more like solving a mystery," offers Anya.

"I like mysteries," says Sinbad.

"Let's start with something simple." I hand out phone books and yearbooks and assorted documents that one of the librarians gathered for us earlier. "Just look for anything that says Korkenderfer."

At first, the whisper and crinkle of turning pages is the only sound we make. Daniel's the first to interrupt the silence. "Hey!" he shouts.

"Dude!" says Josh. "You're in a library!"

"Sorry!" Daniel lowers his voice. "I found something!" He pushes an old phone book toward me.

I put my finger on a fading entry. Charlotte glances over my shoulder and reads aloud. "Rex and Constance Korkenderfer are listed at 1472 Tulip Street in Rockhill."

"Tulip Street is in my neighborhood," says Sinbad. "Were those your grandparents?"

"I don't know," I confess.

"I'll check the *Rockhill Free Press* archives," says Charlotte. "They're all online." It takes less than a minute of swiping on her phone before she's got something to share. "According to Constance Korkenderfer's obituary, she was predeceased by her brother, Ronald, and her husband, Rex. They were married forty-nine years. Constance was the daughter of the late Frank and Theresa Leopold of Providence, Rhode Island. She was survived by a daughter, Wilma Korkenderfer, of Boston, Massachusetts."

"I guess they're my grandparents," I say.

Sinbad reaches across the table and grabs a Rockhill Memorial Cemetery index that's held together by three brass clips in an old green binder. "I can look for them in here."

"Listen to this." Josh takes an old newspaper from the stack in front of him. "Some people say that the Internet is going to change everything."

"Rex and Constance are buried in plot number 3439," Sinbad announces. "They're located in the East Apple section of the cemetery."

"The cemetery has an Apple section?" I ask.

Sinbad unfolds the map that was tucked into the back of the green binder. "It's between the Strawberry section and the Pear section."

"Are we talking about a cemetery or a fruit salad?" says Charlotte.

"Is this really what your dad does for his job?" Daniel asks Anya.

"Sort of," she tells him. "But not really."

"Is your father an FBI agent or something?" asks Josh.

Anya shakes her head. "He's a historian."

Josh holds up his newspaper. "This isn't history. This is real life."

"Josh," says Sinbad. "History is real life."

"Check this out." Daniel pushes a yearbook to the center of the table. "Here's Ellie's mom."

Everybody leans forward to see. On the page, several rows of goofy-looking but surprisingly well-groomed teenagers stare back at us. They're all smiling except one sad-faced boy who's wearing a really ugly sweater. Charlotte notices the sad boy too. "I bet his mother picked that out."

In the bottom corner, a dark-eyed, frizzy-haired girl wearing a sleeveless dress and a big smile tilts her head in a classic yearbook pose. It's Wilma Korkenderfer.

"She looks just like Ellie," says Josh.

"She's definitely the girl we saw on the *CYNDI LAUPER'S NOT DEAD!* website," says Daniel.

Anya studies the photo for a long time. "She's even prettier without all the neon-green eye makeup."

I think so too.

"Have you ever seen a picture of your mother before?" Josh asks me.

I pull the yearbook closer. "Not like this," I admit.

"Is it weird?" he asks.

"No." I change my mind. "It's a little weird." I change my mind again. "Actually, it's very weird."

Charlotte reaches over and flips the yearbook a few pages ahead. She turns the book around so that Anya can check out the photo of a serious, athletic-looking boy. They both start to laugh. "He's still very handsome," says Charlotte.

"Who?" I ask.

"Your dad," says Anya.

I look back and forth between Anya and Charlotte. "You think my father is handsome?"

Charlotte presses the back of her hand to her forehead. "Ellie, your father is the best-looking of all the fathers."

Josh stands. "That's enough history for me."

Over the next few days, my friends and I discover the history of Korky everywhere we look. We visit the Korkenderfers' old house on Tulip Street. We see my grandparents' final resting spots in the cemetery. Both the Korkenderfers and the Magaris are just a few steps away from the happy Buddha. In old yearbooks and fading school newspapers, we find photos and snapshots from my parents' high school days. One picture even shows my parents together after a nighttime football game. Beneath a star-flecked night sky, my teenage dad stands arm in arm with my mother-to-be. Apparently, the Howling Wolves won football games back then. Not only that, my father had hair.

By midweek, my brain is on overload and my head is swimming. Alone in my room on Wednesday night, I sit on my bed and revisit the *CYNDI LAUPER'S NOT DEAD!* website to confirm that the band is still scheduled to play at Trinity College on Friday. They are.

"How are you doing, Ellie?"

I glance up and see my father just outside my room. I didn't even hear him come upstairs.

"Can I ask you a question?" I say.

"Of course."

I put a hand on the shoe box I've been keeping at my bedside table. "How come there's nothing in here about the fact that she got remarried?"

"Are you still going through that box of nonsense?" asks Dad.

"Did she think I already knew?" I ask. "Did she send a wedding invitation that you never gave me?"

Dad stands like a palace guard framed in my doorway. He stares at me without speaking for a long moment. "You were not invited to the wedding," he finally says. "If it makes you feel any better, I'm sure you would have been busy that day."

"Doing what?" I ask.

"Learning how to spell your name? Counting to ten? Pooping in your diaper? I don't know, Ellie. The days were pretty full back then. Of course, Korky wouldn't know about any of that." He turns and heads back downstairs.

Suddenly, I feel an anger grow inside me like an unexpected volcano. If there was a glockenspiel nearby, I would definitely send it sailing toward my father's head. But Dad's not the only person I'm angry at. I'm angry at everybody, and I'm especially angry at myself. Because really, Korky Korkenderfer has not been hiding under deep cover for all these years. If I ever went looking, I probably would have found her. But I didn't go looking. I hardly ever thought about her. I didn't care. I did nothing, and now I have nothing to show for it. Actually, that's not true. I have a box filled with nonsense.

CHAPTER 14: WHO SAYS I'M GOING TO FORGIVE ANYBODY?

The next morning, I find a fat slice of homemade peach cobbler and a tall glass of orange juice on the kitchen table. I eat it, because throwing away good food is stupid. Rather than wait for Daniel, I head to St. Francis alone. I find Sister Stephanie inside the school's front door. "I think I need to see a priest," I tell her.

"Did you do something that requires absolution?" she asks me.

A few lonely students march around us like early-morning zombies bent beneath ten-ton backpacks. "I wanted to commit murder last night."

"Who did you want to kill?"

"Everybody," I confess.

She looks around at the kids plodding past. "Either you changed your mind or more than a few of us survived."

"I didn't follow through."

"Glad to hear it," Sister says. "Let's talk." She turns and heads away, so I follow. We walk into her office, where I take a seat. "So?" she says after closing the door behind us.

"A month ago, I hardly cared about Korky Korkenderfer," I blurt out. "Now I think about her all the time."

Sister Stephanie sits at her desk, leans forward, and rests her chin in her hands. "Can I tell you something about your mother, Ellie?"

"I'm kind of sick of her if you want to know the truth."

"Here's the thing," Sister says. "I don't think you would have liked her."

As a matter of fact, I've come to the same conclusion.

"I remember Wilma," Sister continues. "She liked being popular. She liked to be the center of attention whether she deserved it or not. She was obviously very talented, and from her perspective, talent and good looks meant that she should be the queen bee."

"What did my father like about her?" I ask.

"Your father was a boy," says Sister Stephanie. "Teenage boys often have trouble seeing past a pair of . . ."

"Pretty eyes?" I suggest.

"Sure," says Sister. "Let's go with that. At the same time, your father was not an idiot. He recognized something special in Korky. And he was right. She had talent, she had passion, and she had desire. It was her dream to be a singer, and she wasn't going to quit until she made her dream come true."

"It would have been nice if her dream included being a wife and a mother."

Sister's eyes narrow and she leans toward me across the desk. "First of all," she says, "there are plenty of women in the world whose dream is to have a husband and children. There are also millions of others leading happy, productive, and dare I say blessed lives who are neither married nor maternal."

"I didn't mean anything against conventhood, Sister."

"I'm not just talking about the convent, Ellie."

"I know," I tell her. "It's just that—"

Sister interrupts me. "You know what I always find interesting?"

I have a feeling that she's not actually looking for a reply, so I say nothing.

Sure enough, she continues. "I always find it interesting

that hardly anybody ever criticizes my rock and roll brother for the decisions he's made about his own family life."

I should probably remain silent, but I can't help myself. "Did Mr. Leary leave his wife and kid so he could go and play Cyndi Lauper songs in hotel bars?"

"Actually," Sister tells me, "if you replace the hotel bars with concert arenas and plop the real Cyndi Lauper onstage, then yes. That's exactly what Billy did. And everybody loves him."

"Oh."

"So maybe you need to cut your mother some slack."

"You just said I wouldn't like her."

"When your mother was a girl, she was selfish, self-centered, and self-absorbed. You are your father's daughter, Ellie. You don't put up with that nonsense, which is why I am shopping for a new glockenspiel. That said, I expect your mother matured over the years. For the most part, we all do. But I also expect Korky remained difficult to like for her whole life. Just for different reasons."

"What reasons?" I ask.

"People don't generally appreciate women who decide that they want things for themselves."

That's not what I expected Sister Stephanie to say. "What about my father?" I ask.

In the hallway, the morning bell announces the start of the school day. When the ringing stops, Sister stands and heads for the door. "If you're going to forgive your dead mother, you might as well forgive your dad too. He's a good guy. And he's still here."

I catch up with Sister Stephanie in the doorway. "Who says I'm going to forgive anybody?"

Sister sighs. "Ellie, we all want to be in a story where everybody is nice and nobody hurts and everybody lives happily ever after."

"What's wrong with that?" I ask.

"Nothing is wrong with that. And I can almost guarantee that you're going to get your happy story over and over and over again. I can also guarantee that you're going to get a whole lot more. Both things will be true."

I follow Sister into the hallway, where zombies have been transformed into caffeinated kids rushing to class so they won't be late. "Is this where you tell me not to worry because God will never give me more than I can handle?"

Sister laughs as she joins the crowd of students moving away from me. "Wouldn't it be great if that were true?"

CHAPTER 15: THE THING ABOUT LYING

I don't want to tell Dad about the *CYNDI LAUPER'S NOT DEAD!* concert, which means I have to lie. I've never really lied to my father. Not about big things anyway. As it works out, lying is disturbingly easy. "Anya Flowers asked me to sleep over on Friday night," I tell him after school on Thursday.

"Sure," says Dad, who is in the middle of chopping vegetables at the kitchen counter. "Which one is Anya again?"

Daniel looks up from the homework he's doing at our table. Our Lady of Guadalupe is holding his books open. I expect that both the Blessed Virgin Mary and Daniel know I'm lying right now, so I shoot them a quick just-shut-up look before either one has a chance to speak.

"She's the Polish cookie girl," I remind my dad.

"Her dad is a history professor at Trinity College," adds Daniel.

I forgot that Daniel understands zero parts of just-shut-up.

"Is her father Benjamin Flowers?" Dad grabs one more celery stalk and quickly chops it to bits. "I do a whole medieval bread baking thing with his class every year."

"That's him," Daniel confirms.

Dad slides the chopped veggies from the cutting board into a deep frying pan, where they start to sizzle in hot oil. He grabs a plastic bottle and adds a dash of red-hot Sriracha sauce to the pan. "I'll bake some bread tomorrow. You can bring a couple loaves to share with Benjamin and his family."

"I don't know if I'm going to go," I say.

"Why not?" Dad and Daniel ask at the same time.

Usually, Daniel and I can communicate almost without speaking. Today, however, we do not seem to be working on the same wavelength. If we were in sync, Daniel would understand that I forgot about my father's connection to Dr. Flowers. He'd also see that the relationship between Dr. Flowers and my father is a massive weak spot in this stupid lie.

"Just because," I say.

"Our friends are going to a concert at Trinity College tomorrow night," says Daniel.

Did I mention we are not on the same wavelength?

"Oh?" says Dad, sorting through his spice rack. He doesn't find what he's looking for, so he steps into the walk-in closet we use as a pantry.

I lean toward Daniel and whisper, "What are you doing?"

"Unlike you, I'm trying to tell the truth. But not the whole truth," he adds.

"You're going to get me in trouble!"

"Listen," Daniel says. "You don't have to lie to your father. If it doesn't involve food, he hardly pays attention anyway."

"That's not true," I say.

"Just don't tell him the name of the band, and he'll let you go to the show."

"If he finds out that I want to see *CYNDI LAUPER'S NOT DEAD!*—"

"He won't find out," Daniel promises.

Dad returns to the kitchen with a container of ground ginger. "I guess you see enough of Trinity College already, Ellie. Is that why you don't want to go?"

"We're not going to see the college," Daniel says before I can reply. "We're just going to hear some music and hang out with our friends. Ellie should come."

"If you want, I can give you a ride to campus and pick you up after the concert." Dad gives the vegetables a quick stir. "Then you don't have to go to Anya's."

"No!" Daniel and I say at the same time.

Apparently, we're back on the same page.

"If we go," I say cautiously, "we could take the shuttle."

Trinity College runs a free shuttle around town for anybody with a college ID. Of course, everybody in Rockhill knows that the shuttle drivers never check IDs.

"And then you'll come home after the concert?" Dad adds rice and spice to the frying pan. "Or are you going to sleep at Anya's?"

"I'd rather come home," I tell him.

Dad cracks a couple of eggs and tosses them into the veggie fried rice. "So are you going to the concert or not?"

"I am."

Daniel gives me a big grin.

"Okay," says Dad. "Try to be home by eleven. Also, tell Seamus I say hello."

Neither Daniel nor I say anything for a long moment. Finally, I can't take it any longer. "You don't mind that I'm going?"

"I mind," says Dad. "I mind a lot. But based on these last couple weeks, that's not going to stop you."

"I'm sorry," I say. "It's just—"

"Ellie," says Dad, "you don't need to apologize. You just need to come home safe. You need to know that I always love you, and you need to know that I am liable to behave badly when I worry that somebody might hurt you. Also, in case you haven't noticed, I don't like change."

"I know all those things," I say. "I also know that you are the best dad in the world."

"And the best-looking," says Daniel.

"What?" says Dad.

I cross the room and give my father a hug. "Don't listen to him."

CHAPTER 16: DON'T BACK DOWN

On Friday, it's Sinbad's chance to lead our music class. He starts by passing out chords and words to an old lullaby that most of us already know. It's the one that starts with *Hush, little baby, don't say a word. Mama's gonna buy you a mockingbird.* From there, it turns into a long list of things that go wrong with all the gifts until the baby's got broken glass, and a stubborn goat, and weird dog, and a bunch of junk that makes no sense at all. It could be my theme song.

Sinbad instructs everybody to take out their instruments, except he puts me on the piano at the front of the room. Before we play a note, he counts out a rhythm that is definitely not a lullaby. In four-four time, it goes, ONE and a TWO and a THREE FOUR FIVE, and a ONE and a TWO and a THREE FOUR FIVE. "It's a little like salsa and a little like reggae," Sinbad explains. "But faster, with a more solid beat."

"Dare we call it a Bo Diddley beat?" asks Mr. Leary, who steps into the closet and returns with two cherry-red electric guitars shaped like lightning bolts.

"Whoa," says the class.

Mr. Leary grins. "You ain't seen nothing yet."

He and Sinbad swing the instruments over their shoulders and plug them into small amplifiers parked on the floor. "I made arrangements for each section," Sinbad tells us, "but don't worry if you get lost. It's really just two chords. E and A. Does anybody want to be the singer?"

"ME!" shouts Charlotte. "PICK ME!" She rushes to the front of the room. "I'VE BEEN PRACTICING MY WHOLE LIFE FOR THIS!"

Sinbad glances at Charlotte's brother. "She really has," Josh tells us. "She sings at home all the time."

"How about we let Charlotte sing?" Mr. Leary suggests to Sinbad.

Sinbad nods. "I think that's a good idea." He turns to the class. "Here we go."

With that, he and Mr. Leary hit the E chord. The

rhythm pattern becomes obvious immediately, so the drum line jumps right in. The tune is simple, so our horns and wind sections are right there too. I'm mostly using the piano as a big syncopated metronome to keep everybody in time.

Charlotte, who's standing in the center of the room, offers everybody a grin, opens her mouth, and roars, *"Hush, little baby, don't say a word!"*

Where did that voice come from? I wonder.

"Mama's gonna buy you a mockingbird. And if that mockingbird don't sing . . ."

Charlotte takes a big breath, and Sinbad's guitar fills the space with a sound like *CHUCKA-chucka-chucka-chucka. CHUCKA-chucka-chucka-chucka.* The horn section lays down a big A chord, and our drum line, already loud and fast, picks up the pace and the volume too. Charlotte moves to the next line. *"Mama's gonna buy you a diamond ring. And if that diamond ring turns brass . . ."*

Sinbad continues. *CHUCKA-chucka-chucka-chucka.* Mr. Leary steps forward and slides his left hand down the neck of the guitar so that we hear the sound of train whistles crying and echoing over faraway fields. All in the key of E, then A, then E again. Charlotte jumps back in. *"And if that looking glass is broke, Mama's gonna buy you a billy goat . . ."*

CHUCKA-chucka-chucka-chucka. CHUCKA-chucka-chucka-chucka. This time there's a rising horn section, and now Mr. Leary's guitar sounds almost like he's banging it against a set of church bells. The whole thing is amazing.

All together, we bring the song through the part with the horse and the cart and the bull and the dog and finally the baby has nothing. Charlotte wraps it all up with the final line. *"Hush little baby, don't you cry. Daddy loves you and so do I."*

Sinbad lowers his guitar and turns to Mr. Leary. "What do you think?"

I glance at our teacher, who can't wipe a huge smile off his face. "You've got promise," he tells Sinbad.

After class, Daniel, Charlotte, and Josh begin using the excitement created by our impromptu music room performance to convince as many people as possible to join us at Trinity College to see the *CYNDI LAUPER'S NOT DEAD!* show. By the end of the day, it seems like half the school has decided to be there. Most of them, including Charlotte, Anya, Sinbad, Hannah, and Josh, promise to meet Daniel and me on campus after supper. Still, I'm a little surprised when he and I step aboard the Trinity shuttle bus right after school and find that it's totally empty.

"Where is everybody?" I ask.

"You're it," says the driver, a large woman with a cowboy hat, sunglasses, and graying hair. Daniel and I are both surprised when she asks, "Are you Trinity students?"

Thinking quickly, Daniel sort of ducks the question. "We're going to the concert tonight."

"Really?" says the woman. "Me too."

"You are?" I say.

She nods. "I love Cyndi Lauper."

"The real Cyndi Lauper isn't actually going to be there," I point out.

The driver considers me for a moment. "Honey," she finally says, "you're missing the point."

"That seems to be happening to me a lot lately," I admit.

That gets a smile. A few minutes later, our driver delivers us to the campus gate. "Enjoy the show!" she says.

Daniel and I give her a wave and then head for the cafeteria, where we purchase a couple of pizza slices that taste like notebook paper dipped in canola oil. I can see why the college has accepted Dad's pizza-on-wheels proposal. If they don't do something soon, this kind of pizza could have an effect on enrollment.

In a quiet corner, Daniel and I spread out our textbooks, notes, pencils, and papers, and proceed to knock out most of the homework that's supposed to get done over the weekend. I hear there was a time in the distant past when teachers did not assign weekend homework. The students who learned from those instructors went on to crack the atom, build spaceships, invent the personal computer, win two world wars, and map the human genome. Apparently, that's not good enough anymore.

After a few hours, we pack up our schoolwork and head through the college kitchen to leave our backpacks in Dad's office, which is located near the cafeteria's walk-in coolers. Daniel plops into a chair and examines the line of toy food trucks Dad's arranged like a little parade across his desk. "How soon before your father makes this mobile pizza dream come true?" says Daniel.

"Sooner than you think," I say. "But first it's time for *CYNDI LAUPER'S NOT DEAD!*"

Daniel gets to his feet. "Are you ready?"

I close my eyes and take a deep breath. "I have no idea."

Daniel takes my hand. "Let's find out."

Together, we make our way to the cafeteria's employee exit. The back door puts us a short walk away from the gymnasium where *CYNDI LAUPER'S NOT DEAD!* is supposed to play. It's dark and cold now, so we hurry along with several dozen college kids moving in the same general direction. I know they are only a few years older than me, but it seems like the lives they lead must be so much more interesting and exciting than mine. On the other hand, I'm the one with the rock star for a teacher, a master chef for a dad, and a deceased mom who used to wear neon and zebra stripes to work. I don't know how much more interesting and exciting I could take.

Inside the gym, less than a hundred students have spread across the wooden bleachers. A few more mill around a raised platform parked beneath one of the basketball hoops. I guess that's the stage. Looking around, my St. Francis of Assisi classmates seem to account for more than a quarter of the audience, which leads me to believe that eighties tribute bands might not be the kind of cultural activity most Trinity College students are looking for.

Without warning, the big room drops into sudden darkness. Just as quickly, a portable rack of stage lights illuminates the platform. A moment later, four men and three women jog onstage like all-star athletes ready to take on the world. I recognize most of the band from the website, though honestly, the photographs did not do their outfits justice. I lean toward Daniel. "What were people thinking back then?"

"They were thinking scarves, bracelets, and neon," says Daniel. "Lots and lots of neon." He points at the porkpie lids on the three men who make up the *CYNDI LAUPER'S NOT DEAD!* brass section. "But I do like those hats."

"You'd look good in a porkpie," I assure him.

A tiny girl in a loud, pink tutu and an oversize Betty Boop T-shirt steps up to the microphone. "HELLO, TRINITY COLLEGE!"

"That's original," says a voice in my ear. I turn and find Charlotte standing beside me. In a fluffy red skirt, black fishnet stockings, and a white ruffled pirate blouse, she's dressed as outrageously as the band. Not only that, she's teased her hair into a massive, black lion's mane. Sinbad, wearing a pastel suit, skinny tie, and big white sneakers, stands beside her.

"You really dressed for the occasion," I say.

Before either one of them can reply, the Betty Boop girl, along with two women standing beside her, swing matching pink electric guitars from behind their backs. They bring their instruments around like gunslingers, and in perfect sync with the rest of the band, they launch into a massive power chord that roars through the gymnasium.

"Okay," Charlotte shouts over the guitar harmony. "That was very cool."

The rest of the crowd feels pretty much the same way. The bleachers empty and the whole room is dancing. Not surprisingly, it seems that Sinbad knows all the words to every song. As a matter of fact, so do I. The women onstage take turns singing familiar tunes.

"I think I've memorized their set list!" I holler at Anya and Josh, who are here now too.

"What?" says Josh.

The music is really too loud for conversation, so I just laugh. "Never mind!"

As the show continues, I try to get a good look at the drummer, who's mostly hidden at the back of the platform. When the next song begins, however, the rest of the band steps aside and turns to face the drum kit. "LADIES AND GENTLEMEN!" the lead singer hollers. "GIVE IT UP FOR HOMETOWN BOY MISTER SEAMUS BRADY!"

"Do you know how to play?" Seamus Brady hollers at Charlotte from behind his drum kit.

Charlotte hands the guitar to Sinbad. "We've got this!" she promises.

The backup singer takes a step toward me and then leans into my ear. "You must be Ellie!"

"How do you know?"

"You look just like your mom, which is a good thing because we don't let just anybody up here. Can you sing?"

"I'm better on keyboards," I admit.

She gestures at her partner to switch places. Now it's me playing rhythm on the synthesizer. Sinbad has no problem keeping up on guitar, and Charlotte's jumping up and down alongside the lead singer, who laughs and turns over the mic. On the next downbeat, Charlotte steps up, puts her hands on her hips like she owns the place, and delivers the song's opening lines.

"I come home in the morning light.

My mother says, What you gonna do with your life?

Oh mother dear we're not the fortunate ones . . ."

Seamus nods without smiling, raises a couple of fat sticks, then attacks his drum kit with a quick, steady beat that echoes around the gymnasium like a jackhammer. Betty Boop steps back into the spotlight and shouts over the drumbeat. "THIS ONE IS FOR OUR FRIEND KORKY! I CAN'T SING IT AS WELL AS SHE DID, BUT THIS WAS ONE OF HER FAVORITES. SO HERE GOES!" Horns, keyboards, and bass join the beat along with a twangy guitar hook. The singer wails into the microphone.

"I was minding my business like a good girl should

Just a little too careful for my own good

It was just like living life in the dark

Till something jumped up and it grabbed my heart."

I hear nothing else for a long moment because, honestly, these first few lines just about break me in two. The song could be about me. I was minding my own business. I was living in the dark. And then suddenly, something appeared out of nowhere and grabbed my heart.

The band launches into the chorus.

"I found love. I found real love.

I found love. I found real love . . ."

A wave of sadness rolls over me because this part of the song is not my story. I know I'm surrounded by friends who love me. And my father loves me too. But I wanted more. I wanted to meet my mother. I guess I wanted to be loved by my mother. I'm never going to get that from Wilma "Korky" Korkenderfer.

The rest of the evening flies by in a rush of dance and sweat and music. At one point, I realize that there must be several hundred people inside the gymnasium now. Somehow, the word spread that this is not just a rock and roll show. It's a gospel revival built out of dumb joy. I didn't know a band could do this. The crowd sings and sways and hollers together. Lines from a hundred songs, old and new, get all mashed up in my brain. Then suddenly, all the lights come up to reveal a gymnasium filled with sweaty, laughing friends. More than half the crowd is girls, and Betty Boop earns a roar of approval when she announces the last song of the night. "GIRLS JUST WANT TO HAVE FUN!"

The *CYNDI LAUPER'S NOT DEAD!* horn section launches into a fast-paced, reggae line that's different from the more familiar opening. One of the backup singers moves to an electric keyboard and provides the opening synthesizer chords on top of the brass. Suddenly, Charlotte grabs Sinbad and me by the arms and drags us toward the stage. "What are we doing?" I shout.

"We know this song from marching band!" she hollers.

"So?" I say.

"Follow me!" Charlotte says. "And if they try to stop you, don't back down!"

"Don't back down!" says Sinbad. "Got it!"

"Got it!" I say.

Charlotte grins. "Good!"

Before I know what's happening, Charlotte pulls us on stage with the band. Seamus Brady's eyes open wide when he sees me. "Are you okay?" he shouts.

I point at the sax, the trumpet, and the trombone player blasting away. "I can't hear you!" I lie.

Beside me, Charlotte takes a small white electric guitar off the instrument rack near the base drum, then shoves it toward a microphone with a backup singer who looks shocked but doesn't push me away.

The crowd roars back. *"Girls, they wanna have fun. Oh girls just want to have fun."*

Charlotte steps back like she's been hit by a tidal wave. The room erupts into spontaneous applause. For no apparent reason, I start laughing and crying at the same time. Betty Boop gives Charlotte a big hug, then takes center stage and continues the song. Charlotte leaps off the low platform and rejoins our friends dancing on the gym floor. Just in time, I remember that this song's got a tricky keyboard bridge in the middle. Fortunately, it's not too complicated. When I finish, Betty points at Sinbad, who hops forward and adds a funky guitar solo. I really didn't know he was that good.

As the song moves toward its finish, Betty takes the guitar from Sinbad and gives him a quick kiss on the cheek. The crowd cheers, so Sinbad waves before following Charlotte off stage. The regular keyboardist gives me a nod and a smile, which I understand is my signal to say good-bye too. I take my hands away from the keys, and she slides over without missing a beat. I jog toward the front of the stage, but the lead singer stops me. She takes my arm and lifts it over my head like I'm the new heavyweight champion of the world. While my friends cheer and the music continues, she leans toward me and hollers into my ear. "Stick around after the show!"

I turn and glance at the drummer, who stares back but doesn't acknowledge me.

"Really?" I say.

"Please," Betty Boop tells me. "Say you will."

"Okay," I promise.

Betty pats me on the bottom, grabs the microphone, and moves the song toward its final verses. *"When the working day is done, oh when the working day is done . . ."*

The crowd responds. *"Girls just want to have fun!"*

A few moments later, the show is over. The cheering fades, and the crowd begins to move toward the doors. Daniel, Charlotte, Sinbad, Josh, Anya, and I wander toward the empty bleachers while classmates and college kids move past. A few offer high fives and excited compliments.

"You guys were awesome!"

"That was epic!"

"You rock!"

"We should start our own band!" Charlotte gushes.

"You're already in a band," Anya reminds her.

Charlotte rolls her eyes. "You know what I mean."

My friends start arguing about good names for the band. They've eliminated Corentin and the Quimpers, Shako All Over, The Battle of Pinkie Cleugh, and Hit Me With Your Best Glock by the time the guys from the *CYNDI LAUPER'S NOT DEAD!* horn section spot us and head our way. The trumpet player, a tall African American man still wearing his porkpie hat, sees us and laughs. "Too bad none of you played the horn!"

"The big one plays trombone," a familiar voice offers. "He's pretty good too."

"Ranking Richard!" says the trumpeter.

I turn and see why the voice sounds so familiar. It's because Ranking Richard is Mr. DeGroot.

Daniel hops to his feet. "You!"

Mr. DeGroot holds his hands out. "You're not going to chase me with a zucchini, are you?"

"Why would he chase you with a zucchini?" asks Charlotte.

Mr. DeGroot turns to me. "Or maybe a glockenspiel?"

"What are you doing here?" I ask our old music teacher warily.

"I came to see the show," he says. "And I was hoping to see you too."

Daniel takes out his phone and turns to me. "I'm calling Sister Stephanie."

Honestly, I thought Daniel was going to suggest the police, but Sister Stephanie is probably better.

"Wait," I say. I stand and face Mr. DeGroot. "How did you know I'd be here?"

He shrugs. "I thought you might like to see your mother's band."

"How do you know—"

"Richard," says the trumpet player, who's been joined by the rest of *CYNDI LAUPER'S NOT DEAD!* "You shouldn't have come."

Mr. DeGroot points at me. "You know this is Korky's daughter."

The lead singer, still wearing her Betty Boop T-shirt, steps forward. "We know." She gives me a friendly smile. "You're Ellie, right?"

I nod.

The backup singer who looked so shocked to see me on-stage laughs out loud. "Honey," she says, "when you stepped up to that microphone, I thought I was seeing a ghost." Suddenly, she wraps me in a gigantic hug. "You really do look just like your mother!"

"You all know about me?" I ask after the woman lets me go.

"We know," Betty says again.

I turn to Mr. DeGroot. "Is that why you've been following me around?"

He sticks his hands into his pockets, then takes them out again. "Sort of," he admits.

"Not for revenge?" asks Daniel.

"Revenge?" says Mr. DeGroot. "Revenge for what?"

"For getting you fired?"

Mr. DeGroot shakes his head. "I should send you a thank-you note. I couldn't have lasted in that job another year."

"You were only there for one year," Charlotte reminds him.

"It was the longest year of my life," says Mr. DeGroot. "I hated everything about it. I am not cut out to be a high school teacher."

"I thought you just hated me," says Daniel.

"It was more like strong dislike," Mr. DeGroot tells him.

"Is that supposed to make me feel better?" Daniel asks.

I glance back and forth between Daniel and Mr. DeGroot. "I still don't understand why you're here," I tell our old teacher.

"There's something I want to give you." Mr. DeGroot digs into his coat pocket again. This time he pulls out a couple of old cassette tapes. "These are recordings of your mother singing."

For the first time, Seamus Brady speaks. "Where did you get those?"

"They're mine." Mr. DeGroot shoves the tapes into my hands. "They're from when we were kids."

"Hey!" Sinbad says out of the blue. "He's the Ranking Richard that's on Billy Leary's old album."

"My mom was supposed to sing with you," I say.

Mr. DeGroot nods. "You've been doing your homework. Korky and I were friends for a long time. Of course, that didn't stop her from kicking me out of *CYNDI LAUPER'S NOT DEAD!*"

"You were with the band?" I ask.

"Korky and I named the band," Mr. DeGroot says proudly.

"Then why did she kick you out?"

Seamus Brady steps forward to answer my question. "We play hundreds of shows every year. We're on the road all the time. It is a good life if you like it, but you have to be like a family. Richard forgot the part about family."

"You don't fire your family," says Mr. DeGroot.

"A family keeps its promises," says Seamus.

Mr. DeGroot's face turns a familiar, angry red. "It was a stupid promise."

"Nobody asked you whether or not it was stupid," Seamus says. "Korky simply asked—"

"Korky asked us to keep a secret that wasn't good for anybody." Mr. DeGroot's voice rises. "How did that make any sense?"

"She wanted to handle things her own way," offers the Betty Boop singer in a calmer voice.

"Her way of handling things was to pretend she was never going to die," Mr. DeGroot shouts. "How did that work out?"

"Richard," says the tall horn player. "Nobody is happy about the way things worked out."

"Mr. DeGroot," Daniel says calmly. "Does this secret you're talking about have something to do with Ellie?"

I was wondering the same thing, but I didn't want to ask. As Dad likes to say, not everything is about you. But sometimes it is.

I tuck the two cassette tapes into my pockets. "Does it?" I ask.

"Seamus," says Mr. DeGroot, "she's already figured most of it out. Would you please tell her the rest?"

Seamus Brady shakes his head. "I keep my promises."

This man sounds a lot like my dad.

Betty Boop puts an arm around my shoulder. "Ellie," she says, "Korky really wanted to meet you one day. But as time went on, she got more and more afraid that she'd waited too long. And then she got sick. And then Richard sent you the box."

"Richard?" I say. "You mean Mr. DeGroot?" I turn and face our old teacher. "You sent me the shoe box?"

Mr. DeGroot nods.

I glance around at the members of the band. Under the harsh, yellow gymnasium lights, they look more like tired Walmart employees than rock and roll stars. "I don't understand," I say. "My mother didn't send me anything?"

Mr. DeGroot glances at Seamus, who says nothing. "Fine," says Mr. DeGroot. "This is what happened. Korky talked about getting in touch with you for years, but she kept putting it off. When she got sick, she made us promise that we wouldn't tell you or your dad."

"Why?" I ask.

"There is no right answer to that question." Mr. DeGroot

says the words to me, but it's clear that he means them for his former bandmates. "She should have called you a long time ago, but she didn't. And then we learned that she might only have a few months to live. I thought if I sent you a few things first, then Korky would—"

"You tried to trick her into calling me?" I say.

"It's more like I was trying to force her hand."

"Is that your handwriting inside the box lid?" I ask.

Mr. DeGroot hesitates for a moment. "When I told Korky how I added those 'Time after Time' lyrics—" He shakes his head. "That's what really got me fired."

"She was very angry," Betty Boop offers quietly.

Mr. DeGroot sighs. "It was not a good day."

I am surprised by Anya, who steps forward and takes my hand. "It was not your job to choose the first words that Ellie would hear from her mother," she informs Mr. DeGroot.

"Korky should have picked those words herself," says Seamus Brady.

"I agree," says Mr. DeGroot, "but—"

I finish the sentence. "But she never did."

For a long moment, nobody speaks. Finally, Betty whispers, "She just ran out of time."

Seamus Brady lowers himself onto a wooden bleacher

and places his head in his hands. "At the end, there was no time for anything. Some days she felt good. Some days were terrible. There were so many bills and appointments. Plus, she insisted that we keep the band going."

"Because we are a family," says one of the horn players.

Seamus looks up at the man. "I didn't always know the right thing to do."

"Not like now," offers the singer who welcomed me on-stage. "Now everything is crystal clear. Right, honey?"

Even Seamus laughs a little at that. Confusion might be nothing new, but apparently nobody's getting any better at dealing with it.

"She didn't plan to die," I say out loud.

"She sort of planned to live forever," Betty Boop tells me.

"In the long run," says Mr. DeGroot, "that wasn't a good plan."

Nobody replies until Charlotte suddenly speaks up. "Seriously? Didn't you all go to Catholic school? Did you listen to anything good old St. Francis had to say? Be an instrument of peace? Treat animals kindly and people at least as well? For it is in giving that you receive? If you ask me, Ellie's mom should have paid closer attention to that last bit." She turns to Seamus. "Did Korky skip that class in high school?"

It's clear that Seamus doesn't really know how to respond. "Back in high school—"

An unexpected thought enters my head along with a sudden stab of fear. "You're not my real dad, are you?"

Seamus Brady looks up. "Of course not. Bruce Magari is your dad. He is a good man."

I stare at Seamus Brady without speaking. It strikes me that I've spent the last two weeks rummaging through shoe boxes and music and history and confusion. I've dragged everybody along in this quest for some true thing that I can know about my family. Something that will always be mine. Something that will never change. And there it is.

"You're right," I say. "He really is."

CHAPTER 17: HER LOSS

I find my father in the kitchen. He's turning a batch of flour and water into dough on the counter, which is not unusual except for the fact that it's after midnight. "I'm sorry I'm late," I say.

"I figured I'd do something while I waited up." Dad continues working the dough without turning to face me. "What's your excuse?"

"We stayed and talked to the people in the band."

"That's what I expected." At the counter, Dad presses his fingers into the wet mixture, which begins to change into something new in his hands.

"You're not mad?"

"I'm glad you got a chance to meet them."

I take a seat at the kitchen table and realize that Daniel and I forgot our backpacks in Dad's office. "By the way," I say, "I told Daniel that the pizza bus is coming soon. He wants to be your sous chef."

"Daniel watches too many cooking shows." Dad continues kneading dough.

"Did you know the shoe box didn't really come from Korky Korkenderfer?" I ask after a long moment.

"I had a feeling." Dad rolls his dough into a large ball, places his palms on top of it, and then presses down with all his weight. Once it spreads out, he folds the dough, turns it over, and repeats the process. "It wasn't her style."

"What was her style?" I ask.

"She wasn't subtle. She didn't leave mysterious clues. She was all in or all gone. She would have appreciated the glockenspiel throw."

"Everybody says I look like her."

"You do." Dad pulls a tiny pinch of dough off the ball and pops it into his mouth. After a brief pause, he continues kneading. "Was Mr. DeGroot at the concert tonight?"

"He was there."

"That must have been interesting." Dad tastes another bit of dough and decides the kneading is done. "Good old

Ranking Richard should have respected your mother's wishes."

"So you know everything?"

"Only because I gave Seamus Brady a call earlier today. I asked him to keep an eye out for you tonight. He filled me in on the other stuff." Dad grabs a bench knife, which is basically a big stainless-steel rectangle attached to a wooden handle. He uses the tool to scrape the dough off the counter and transfer it to a deep ceramic bowl.

"Is that for pizza?" I ask.

"It's bread dough." Dad covers the bowl with a dish towel, then moves it to the refrigerator. "I'll bake fresh loaves in the morning. You can bring one to Anya's family."

"She didn't ask me to sleep over," I say. "I lied. I'm sorry."

"Let me guess," Dad says while he washes his hands. "You lied because you thought I wouldn't let you go to the concert."

"Pretty much," I admit.

"But then you changed your mind once I was okay with it."

"Yes, but I still didn't want to tell you we were going to see *CYNDI LAUPER'S NOT DEAD!*"

Dad grabs a towel to dry his hands. "I always hated that name. The only band that should have Cyndi Lauper's name in it is Cyndi Lauper's band." He returns the towel to a hook. "Don't lie to me again, okay?"

I nod. "Can I ask you a question?"

Dad takes a seat beside me at the table. "Of course."

"Why didn't you give me the shoe box right away?"

Dad shakes his head. "When that box arrived, I knew something wasn't right. If Korky wanted you to have that stuff, she would have come here and handed it to you herself. I figured I'd put it away and save it and see what happened next." Dad pauses for a moment, then adds, "She never came."

"Because she died," I point out.

"Yes," Dad says. "She died. She died without ever getting in touch with her own daughter."

I recall what Betty Boop said after the concert. "She didn't think she had enough time to do it right."

"So what?" Dad's voice rises. "So what if she'd done a rotten job of it? At least she would have tried. That would have been better than doing nothing."

"That's almost the same thing Mr. DeGroot said."

Dad shrugs. "Even an idiot gets it right sometimes."

"I'm not sure he's an idiot," I tell my father.

"Ellie," says Dad, "the man made my ex-wife so angry that she basically excommunicated him from her life. After that, he got my daughter so upset that she tried to turn a glockenspiel into a harpoon."

"Well, there's that," I admit.

Dad pushes his chair away from the table. "I reserve the right to think that he's an idiot."

"Can I ask one more question?"

"It's way past my bedtime," Dad points out.

"This is an easy one," I promise.

Dad sighs. "Okay."

"Are you still mad at me?" I ask.

Dad looks up at the ceiling. "I don't think I was ever really mad at you, Ellie."

"I thought we weren't go to lie to each other," I tell my father.

"Maybe I was a little mad at you," he admits. "Mostly, I was mad at your mother." Dad shakes his head. "I thought I was done being angry at Korky, but apparently that woman can still wind me up after all these years, and even from beyond the grave."

"You must have loved her a lot."

"In the end, that's why I gave you the box," Dad tells me. "I wanted her to be part of your life." He pauses before adding, "I really wanted her to be part of our life together."

"But that didn't happen," I say.

"No," Dad says. "It didn't."

Dad shakes his head. And that's when I know for sure that this isn't going to be one of those stories where I discover some deep and meaningful connection with the long-lost mother I never had. Wilma Korkenderfer gave me life, big feet, frizzy hair, and not much else. And that's just how it's going to be.

Dad reaches across the table and takes my hand. "Her loss," he says.

CHAPTER 18: EVERYTHING IS BETTER WITH A SOUNDTRACK

In late November, Seamus Brady calls to ask if Dad and I would like to be with him when he places Korky's ashes in the cemetery plot where my grandparents are buried. "We'll be there," I promise.

"So they cremated her after all?" Daniel says when I call to let him know about the plans.

"That's not what matters," I tell him. "Are you going to help me or not?"

"You know that you can count on me."

Daniel's right. I do know.

Just after Thanksgiving, Seamus, Dad, and I meet at the cast-iron cemetery gate at the end of our street. Together we follow the winding path past the laughing Buddha. We stop a few yards away in front of the marble stones etched with the names of my grandparents, Rex and Constance Korkenderfer.

"Did Korky like her parents?" I ask.

"She did," says Seamus, who I've discovered is not a particularly talkative man. "But they didn't always see eye to eye."

"I hope they work things out," I tell him. "They're going to be together for a long time."

I hand Dad a garden spade we borrowed from Daniel's garage. He pushes it into the dry grass between the two Korkenderfer headstones. Using the flat blade, he cuts a medium-size square into the sod, which we roll back like a piece of old carpet. While Dad continues to remove dirt from the exposed patch of soil, Seamus takes a plastic bag filled with gray ash out of the big cardboard box he's been carrying close to his chest.

"Hi, Mom," I say to the bag.

Both Seamus and Dad shoot me dirty looks.

"Sorry," I say.

Dad turns back and deepens the hole a bit more.

"Where have you been keeping her?" I ask Seamus.

"On the kitchen counter," he confesses.

He must notice the shocked look on my face.

"Korky always liked to watch me cook," he explains. "She said she married me for my cooking."

At that, Dad gives the earth an especially hard stab with the spade. Seamus and I exchange a quick glace and decide to end that conversation for now. Dad straightens and gestures at the ground. "That should do it."

Without speaking, Seamus opens the bag and pours its contents into the hole. Dad hands him the shovel so he can complete the work. Unexpectedly, Seamus turns the spade over to me.

"Are you sure?" I ask.

"I'm sorry she never met you," Seamus says. "Now go ahead and put her to rest."

I take the spade, move dirt on top of Korky Korkenderfer's ashes, then roll the sod back into place. The entire operation takes less than five minutes. Now almost no evidence exists that anything's happened here at all, which is probably for the best since, technically, I think that adding an extra dead person to an existing gravesite is not allowed.

I hand the shovel to Dad and turn to Seamus. "If you don't mind, there's something I'd like to leave here."

Seamus nods, so I take the backpack I've been carrying over my shoulders and place it at my feet. Inside the bag, I've got the Our Lady of Guadalupe statue that used to live just a few feet away. I remove the ceramic figure and place it on the piece of grass that covers Korky's remains.

"That's good," says Seamus.

"There should be something to mark the spot," Dad agrees.

I have to move some spare dirt against the base to prevent Mary from falling on her face, but finally she stands without my help. The statue's earned several new chips and scuff marks since Halloween. So have I. And I'll survive.

Seamus Brady reaches into his cardboard box once more. This time he takes out an old, black portable stereo. It's got a long handle across its top and a cassette player built into its middle. "For you," he tells me. "You can use it to play those tapes that Richard gave you."

The cassettes from Mr. DeGroot are stacked neatly on a shelf in my room. I still haven't listened to them yet. I'd planned to be by myself when I played them for the first time. But now that I think about it, it will be better if I am surrounded by people I love. I really hope Dad will be part of it, but I'm pretty sure he's not ready yet.

"Thank you," I say.

Seamus nods, then turns back toward Korky's simple grave.

"There's one more thing," I say.

"Oh?" says Seamus.

"It didn't seem right to do this without music, so I asked my friends to help me put something together."

Seamus gives a small nod. "Korky used to say that everything is better with a soundtrack."

I glance at Dad, who looks a little confused. "You better cover your ears," I say.

"Why?" he asks.

I take a silver drum major whistle out of my pocket, put it to my lips, and blow till my own ears ring. "That's why."

A moment later, the St. Francis of Assisi Marching Band, including every member of *CYNDI LAUPER'S NOT DEAD!*, appears from behind Mr. Leary's barn, which is just a few yards away. Mr. Leary himself is marching a snare drum today. Hannah Shupe, Sister Stephanie, and a very enthusiastic drum line lead the Howling Wolves around the cemetery like a New Orleans funeral parade. "Hey!" I yell at Mr. Leary when he marches past. "Are you going to be our teacher for the rest of the year?"

"If my sister lets me!" he calls back.

Finally, when the band's got me, Dad, and Seamus surrounded, Hannah raises one hand, makes a fist, and draws it down, signaling a full stop. The instruments fall silent. That's when the *CYNDI LAUPER'S NOT DEAD!* horn section moves to the front of the line.

I grab my father's shoulder and whisper into his ear. "Give me a hand."

With Dad's assistance, I struggle to the top of my grandparents' gravestones. I place one foot on Rex and the other on Constance. I cup both hands around my mouth and yell to the band. "Ready!"

"Ready!" they respond.

I count off. "ONE! TWO! THREE! FOUR!"

The horn section rips into a massive chord. I knew it would be good, but I didn't know it could be this good. Seamus Brady's eyes go wide. I nearly tumble off my grandparents and onto the top of Our Lady of Guadalupe, but my father saves me. While I'm finding my feet, the band launches into the familiar opening of Cyndi Lauper's "Girls Just Want to Have Fun."

"Did you do this?" yells Seamus, who seems awestruck by the whole thing.

I grin and nod. "My father said Korky didn't appreciate subtle."

"She really would have liked you, Ellie."

"It's nice to hear that," I tell him.

It's true. I really am happy that the people who knew my mother best think she would have liked me. I hope they're right. I hope she might have even loved me. And who knows? Maybe she already did. But for better or worse, she never told me. She never did a thing about it.

Her loss.

ACKNOWLEDGMENTS

Some years ago, I met the kind, talented, and very generous Laurie Halse Anderson. Back then, she asked me about my children, who were very young. "They are going to grow," Laurie warned me. "That's going to change you. That's going to change the stories you tell. Don't fight it."

Thank you to Laurie for the warning and the very good advice. Most especially, thank you to my now young-adult children—Gabrielle and Nicholas—for inspiring me every day.

As a father to a teenage daughter, I've been thinking a lot about forces that help and hinder girls. Thank you to family, friends, artists, teachers, preachers, and mentors who, through your work, your words, and your example encourage and inspire girls everywhere to choose paths that are brave, happy, healthy, and smart.

That brings me to Cyndi Lauper. It has been a joy to spend so much time with this woman's voice in my head. In her music, in her writing, and in the important and beautiful work she does for young people and adults, she's got a lot to say. People should listen.

On a separate note, I'd like to get one thing straight: this book is not about my mother. My mom has never fronted a rock and roll band (though she does have a really pretty singing voice), she's never gone missing, and her fashion choices are not inspired by Cyndi Lauper. That said, I have a feeling that my mom and Ms. Lauper would like each other a lot. If anybody can make that meeting happen, please give me a call.

As always, I have an army of family, friends, and colleagues who encourage and support my storytelling habit. I deeply appreciate every one of you, especially my wife, Debbie, who I fall in love with every day.

Special thanks go to my agent, Susan Hawk, and my editor, Nancy Mercado. Having you both in my life makes me a better writer and a better person. It is also a special treat for me to be part of both the Upstart Crow and the Scholastic families.

Finally, thank you to readers everywhere for making books and stories a necessary part of life.

ABOUT THE AUTHOR

Paul Acampora has written four novels and people have said really nice things about each of them. Kids, parents, and critics praise his work for its laugh-out-loud humor, rollicking dialogue, and heartfelt exploration of what it means to be human. Of his most recent novel, *How to Avoid Extinction*, School Library Journal said, "A cast of memorable characters, intelligent banter, and wry humor reminiscent of Richard Peck or Gary Paulsen make this an authentic and unforgettable journey." You can find Paul online at paulacampora.com.